W9-AYL-444

John and Margaret were picnicking beside the Black Forest when a weeping man in an ancient costume walked past. . . .

"He looked so strange," said John. "Not just his clothes. Himself."

"He didn't even see us. We might as well not have been here at all!" said Margaret.

"Something awful must have happened to him," whispered John. "Not just an accident, or getting hurt—but something really awful."

"Like having a wound deep inside and bleeding to death slowly, but not telling anyone!"

John looked doubtful, then nodded. The man was in some terrible trouble. He had vanished into the shadows of the forest just as if he had been a dream, or a ghost. It seemed wrong to let him pass like that, and go his way to suffer alone, without even offering to help.

Not, of course, that there was anything that they could do. All the same . . .

Fawcett Crest Books
by Mary Stewart:

- ☐ AIRS ABOVE THE GROUND 23868 $1.95
- ☐ THE GABRIEL HOUNDS 23946 $2.25
- ☐ THE IVY TREE 23976 $2.25
- ☐ MADAM, WILL YOU TALK? 23250 $1.95
- ☐ THE MOON SPINNERS 23941 $2.25
- ☐ MY BROTHER MICHAEL 24029 $2.25
- ☐ NINE COACHES WAITING 23988 $2.25
- ☐ THIS ROUGH MAGIC 24129 $2.25
- ☐ THUNDER ON THE RIGHT 23940 $2.25
- ☐ TOUCH NOT THE CAT 23201 $2.25
- ☐ WILDFIRE AT MIDNIGHT 24008 $2.25

And the Merlin Novels:

- ☐ THE CRYSTAL CAVE 24111 $2.95
- ☐ THE HOLLOW HILLS 24112 $2.95
- ☐ THE LAST ENCHANTMENT 24207 $2.95

Buy them at your local bookstore or use this handy coupon for ordering.

COLUMBIA BOOK SERVICE (a CBS Publications Co.)
32275 Mally Road, P.O. Box FB, Madison Heights, MI 48071

Please send me the books I have checked above. Orders for less than 5 books must include 75¢ for the first book and 25¢ for each additional book to cover postage and handling. Orders for 5 books or more postage is FREE. Send check or money order only.

Cost $_____	Name _____
Sales tax*_____	Address _____
Postage_____	City _____
Total $_____	State _____ Zip _____

*The government requires us to collect sales tax in all states except AK, DE, MT, NH and OR.

MARY STEWART

A Walk in Wolf Wood

A Tale of Fantasy and Magic

FAWCETT CREST • NEW YORK

A WALK IN WOLF WOOD

Published by Fawcett Crest Books, a unit of CBS Publications, the Consumer Publishing Division of CBS Inc., by arrangement with William Morrow & Company, Inc.

Copyright © 1980 by Mary Stewart

ALL RIGHTS RESERVED

ISBN: 0-449-24433-4

Printed in the United States of America

First Fawcett Crest Printing: August 1981

10   9   8   7   6   5   4   3   2   1

FOR JASON, ELINOR, JENNIFER

AND CHARLES

A Walk in Wolf Wood

CHAPTER ONE

John and Margaret Begbie were sitting on a rug beside a track through the Black Forest in Germany when a man walked past them, weeping bitterly.

The children and their parents had been having a picnic. They had left the car in a parking area beside the road, and, carrying the rug and the picnic things, walked back to where a wide track led steeply downwards from the road into the shade of the trees at the forest's edge. Between track and roadway was a wedge-shaped stretch of mossy grass, where an old, battered wooden signpost stood, and near it the mossed stump of an enormous tree. They spread the rug beside this, full in the sun. To their left the track led on steeply downhill, to vanish into the darkness of the forest. Ahead of them the trees grew more thinly, giving sunlit glimpses of the wooded valley below. A river ran there, and there, on its rocky hill, stood the ruined castle that the Begbie family had visited that morning. They could see, tiny in the distance, the narrow wooden bridge that spanned the dry moat, and the hut where they had bought tickets and postcards. Beyond the castle was the glint of water where the river ran. Beyond that again, and wherever the eye could travel, were trees, trees and more trees....

The forest was very quiet. The children's father, drowsing after the meal, lay full length beside them, asleep. Mrs. Begbie had gone back to the car; for her knitting, she said, but she had been gone so long that the children suspected that she, too, had dozed off in the sleepy heat of the afternoon. No cars had gone by; no one had passed that way at all, until the strange man came down the track from the roadway. He walked quickly, head down, and, though he passed within a yard of them, took no notice at all of the two children and their father.

John and Margaret stared after him, surprised and disturbed. They had never seen a grown man cry before, and besides, this man did not seem to mind who saw or heard him. His breathing shuddered, and he stumbled now and then as if his tears blinded him, but he made no attempt to wipe them away. They poured down his face and dripped onto the faded red velvet of his coat.

That was another strange thing about him: the way he was dressed. He was the wrong age, and looked the wrong kind of man, to be wearing the rather flamboyant costume he had on. A long tunic of crimson velvet—like a close-fitting coat—clothed him to the thighs. It was buttoned all down the front with gilded buttons, and girded low on the hips with a studded belt of worked leather. Below it he wore some kind of leggings, or hose, of faded grey-blue, and shoes of soft, scuffed-looking brown leather. Over it all went a cloak of the same grey-blue as the hose. This had a hood which had been pushed back to hang behind over his shoulders, like a collar. He went bareheaded. His clothes, odd though they were, gave the impression of once having been very good, and very expensive; but they were sadly shabby now.

"A knife, too." John spoke softly, so as not to wake Mr. Begbie. "Did you see? He had a long knife at his belt."

"Well, yes," said Margaret, "but it's just part of the costume, isn't it? Remember those dancers we watched the other evening at St. Johann, doing the local dances in peasant costume? The men were wearing knives like that. It won't be real. Not for use, I mean."

"I suppose not, but his clothes didn't look a bit like those peasant costumes. For one thing, they were sort of shabby, as if he wore them every day. As if he was used to them. The

dancers we saw, well, they were just dressing up. You could tell," he finished, rather feebly.

"Could he be a forester, or something?"

"I don't know. Did you see the chain round his neck, with that big medallion thing on it? It looked like gold. Why would a forester—or anyone, come to that, who isn't a pop star—wear a thing like that?"

"Imitation, to go with the costume."

"But it wasn't costume. I told you—"

"Imitation, anyway," said Margaret decidedly. "It couldn't be gold, not a thing that size. It would be worth a fortune, and he didn't look rich."

"No, but he didn't look like a peasant, either," said John obstinately. "He reminded me of something, but I can't remember what. Whoever he was, he looked..." He paused again, searching for the right description, and failed to find it. "He looked so strange," was all he could think of. "Not just his clothes. Himself."

"He was crying, you mean," said Margaret. "He didn't even see us. We might as well not have been here at all."

The children looked at one another. Beside them Mr. Begbie stirred in his sleep, but did not waken. It was very quiet. A wood pigeon flew out of the high treetops with a clap and flurry of wings. A jay screamed in the distance, and from time to time a wren flew down onto the ferns nearby, with a shrill, cross little song. But otherwise the forest was still, with the heavy, sleepy stillness of summer.

Not that it was really silent. If you lay with your eyes shut, and really tried to listen to the silence, you could hear it; it was made up of thousands of tiny sounds which might be the trees growing, or the toadstools pushing up through the pine needles, or the air breathing gently through the twigs overhead as the sun heated the ground and the moisture drifted upwards from the mosses. Then there were the insects; under and over and through all the silence was a steady throbbing hum that was so much a part of the forest that it seemed to be inside the listener's brain, and not outside in the wood. It was made of the wingbeats of millions of tiny insects, gnats, bees, wasps, hover flies. The forest hummed silently, and the still air vibrated.

The children heard nothing of the immense secret life of the forest. They were still staring at one another, and, as sometimes happens with people who know each other very well, each of them sensed what the other was thinking.

"Something awful had happened to him," whispered John. "Not just an accident, or getting hurt—and anyway there was no sign of that—but something really awful."

"Like having a wound, deep inside," said Margaret, "and bleeding to death slowly, but not telling anyone."

John, who was older, and perhaps less imaginative, looked doubtful, then nodded. It must be certainly true that the man was in some bad trouble, so bad that he seemed hardly to know what he was doing or where he was going. He had vanished into the shadows of the forest as if he had been a dream, or a ghost. But they could not get him out of their minds. It seemed wrong just to let him pass like that, and go his way to suffer alone, without even offering help.

Not, of course, that there was anything they could do. All the same...

"We could go just a little way," suggested Margaret, "just to see where he was going."

She did not say why, and John did not question it. Neither of them could afterwards explain why it suddenly seemed so urgent that they should follow the stranger into the wood. In the normal way they would have been thankful that he had not noticed them, and would have kept out of his way until he had recovered himself, but now a kind of compulsion seemed to seize them. Margaret was already on her feet. John, though usually the more cautious of the two, hesitated only briefly before he followed suit.

"All right, but we ought to wake Daddy and tell him."

They thought about it for a moment or two. Mr. Begbie was really very fast asleep indeed, and they remembered vividly the times when they had, by mistake, woken him up and met the blast of his wrath, and their mother's exasperated reasoning: "Your father works very hard and needs to rest. Leave him alone, now, children, do, and go and play quietly somewhere else...."

"I don't think we'd better," whispered Margaret. "At any rate, not until we're quite sure there's something wrong. They're always telling us not to disturb him when he's catching up on his sleep, and sending us away. And they did both tell us to go for a walk this afternoon."

"But not to go far."

"Well, it might not be far. And it'll be obvious which way we've gone. There's only the one track."

"Well, all right, but you know what we're supposed to do. We'll leave a note telling them where we've gone. Where's that pencil and pad you were drawing with?"

So, very sensibly, that was what they did. John wrote: "Have gone down this track to explore. J and M." They put the note on the tree stump where the picnic basket stood, weighted it down with a corner of the basket, and then, very quietly, so as not to rouse Mr. Begbie, they tiptoed past the sleeping figure on the rug, and followed the track downhill into the forest.

CHAPTER TWO

The track led fairly steeply downhill for some distance, then levelled out as it curved deeper into the forest. Here the trees crowded more closely together, immensely tall, each one trying to push up beyond the others to reach the light. There were no oaks or beeches any more, no brambles and ferns and harebells beside the track; only the smooth, straight trunks of the pines, like pillars holding up the black thatch of boughs that shut out the sunshine as effectively as a roof. Even the floor of the forest grew no more moss, but it did grow things more colourful and more exciting. Everywhere among the tree roots and thick fallen needles were clusters of toadstools. White eggs pushed up to become weird-looking stinkhorns; brown balls opened out into bronze and lilac wood blewits; and here and there, looking like illustrations to a story about Elfland, were scarlet caps spotted with white, the poisonous fly agarics.

"Don't touch them," warned John, as his sister stopped to look closer.

"I'm not going to! It's funny, isn't it, how these are always the ones in the storybooks, with gnomes and things sitting on them? Just because they're so pretty, I suppose, but really when you look closely at some of the others, they're just as pretty. Hey, John."

"What?"

"Ought we to go back now? We seem to have been walking for ages, and there's no sign of him."

"Perhaps we ought. Look, there's a tree lying across the track at that bend there. Let's just go as far as that."

The tree he spoke of was a huge, fallen pine which lay some distance off, clear across the way. They ran towards it. Beyond the fallen trunk the track seemed to plunge even deeper into the forest. It was like a black tunnel between black pillars.

John kicked at the dead twigs and broken stuff that lay under the trunk. "He must have come this way. It's the only path. He'd have an awful job to make his way round all this—oh, no, here's where he climbed over. There's a footmark in the soft stuff, and—did he have a dog with him? I didn't see one."

"Nor did I." Margaret came to his elbow, peering. There was the footmark, deep and distinct in the soft earth, and another, a pace from it, less distinct. With these, equally clear, were pawprints, big ones, even bigger than the prints that Tray made. Tray was their dog, who had had to be left at home. He was an Alsatian.

"Then it's probably a wolf," said John cheerfully. He grabbed at a branch above his head, and began to clamber up onto the fallen trunk. "Yes, he got over here, there's some mud on the trunk. There ought to be wolves here, of course! Perhaps that's why he carried the long knife."

Margaret looked round her uneasily. She knew quite well that John was joking, but somehow, in this enormous, dark and silent forest, the idea of wolves did not seem strange at all. "What do you mean, there ought to be?"

John, balancing on the tree trunk, grinned down at her. "Don't you remember, when Daddy was planning the picnic, they were looking at the map, and he said that this wood was called Wolfenwald?"

Margaret looked blank, because, though the name Wolfenwald looks very like "wolf" when you see it written on a map, it is actually pronounced, in German, "Volfenvalt."

"Well," she began, "I don't see—"

"It means Wolf Wood," said John flatly.

"Oh."

"It said it on the signpost, too. Didn't you notice?"

"No."

"So he'd have to carry a knife."

"But if there really are wolves here," said Margaret reasonably, "why not a gun?"

"With that costume? A bow and arrow would suit it better! I've remembered what he reminded me of now. It's— Here, hang on a minute!" John stopped abruptly, and began to scramble down on the far side of the tree.

"What is it?"

"Look, Meg, can you get over? Come and see. It's all right, I was only joking about the wolves. Only, can you get across, quickly?"

Margaret soon clambered up after him, and dropped down on the other side of the tree trunk. John was standing among the welter of fallen branches. He pointed down among them. She looked. There, shining among the broken stuff and dead pine needles, was a big gold medal and a tumble of gold chain.

She found herself speaking in a whisper. "When he climbed over the tree trunk, it must have caught on something, and with him crying like that—"

"He wouldn't even notice when he lost it," finished John. He stooped and picked the thing up, balancing it in his hand. "It's pretty heavy, it could have swung forward as he bent over, and slipped off somehow. See, the chain's not broken or anything."

"What's on the medal?"

John held it out on his palm. The children looked at it. It shone so brightly that, even in the dim light of the forest, they could see it quite clearly. It was like a big coin. In the center was a man's head, a young face, in profile, with hair down to the shoulders. He wore a narrow circlet, like a crown. Below the portrait was what seemed to be a name: OTHO. They turned the medallion over. Across the back was the single word FIDELIS.

"The man we saw wasn't Otho," said John. "He's quite different, and older anyway. *Fidelis* is Latin, I do know that. It's in our school motto. It means 'faithful.'"

Margaret fingered the chain. It was beautifully made, heavy but flexible, each link finely engraved. "I think it's real," she said, awed. "Real gold. It's so heavy. Gold's heavy, isn't it? I know Mummy's gold bracelet weighs an awful lot."

John balanced the thing again in his hand. "It is heavy, yes. If it's real—" He looked round him at the silent forest, at the track vanishing round a curve into darkness.

"If it's real," said Margaret, "it's terribly valuable. But even if it isn't, he'll want it back. Perhaps we ought to go on and try to catch him up?"

John nodded. "He's probably missed it by now, anyway, and he'll be on his way back. We'll go just a bit farther. We can't very well leave it here, hanging from the tree. If it *is* real, then anybody could pick it up, or anything. Jays take shiny things, don't they, and magpies? I did hear a jay farther back in the wood."

"All right. But let's run, shall we? It—it's beginning to get dark."

"That's only because the trees are so thick here. It's hours still till sunset. Don't worry. We'll just go as far as that bend, and if we don't see him coming back we'll go back ourselves."

"And the medal?" asked Margaret.

"We'll give it to Daddy. He'll know what to do. Leave it with the police, or something. Come on, then."

They ran on. The bend, when they got to it, wasn't really a bend, just a curve, with another bend beyond that. And another...The track narrowed, twisting deeper between the trees. Roots webbed the paths, like snares made of rope. It was certainly growing darker. Margaret tripped, saved herself, and stopped. John had not noticed. Running slightly ahead of her, he was already out of sight.

"John! John! Let's go back now!"

Silence. She realized, suddenly, that she could no longer hear her brother's footsteps. But before she had time to feel scared, she heard him calling. "Meg! Here it is! It's all right, there's a house here! Come and see!"

She ran to catch up with him. He was waiting for her in a patch of rosy sunlight that shone through a gap in the trees, like a spotlight on a dark stage. The gap was to the right of the track. There, down between the trunks, a little path curved towards a clearing, where the sun, pouring in, had allowed mosses to grow, and ferns, and brambles and even flowers. And some of the flowers were garden ones; gone a bit wild, perhaps, as the garden had.

For there was, indeed, the remains of a garden. It lay around a small cottage, so small, so mossed and weed-grown, with walls and thatch so exactly the colour of the forest, and merging with the fading light, that it was a marvel they had seen it at all.

"I'll bet that's his house," said John. "He was just on his way home."

"And a fine old welcome he'd get!" said his sister. "Just look at it! Those aren't curtains at that window, they're cobwebs, and the door's not been opened for years!"

John looked at it doubtfully. "People always use the back door in the country."

"There's no smoke from the chimney, either."

"Well, on a day like this? Anyway," said John briskly, "we've got to try and return this gold thing. Even if this isn't his house, the people may know who he is, and we can leave it with them. Come on."

They picked their way through the long weeds and brambles. There was a knocker on the cottage door. It was rusty with neglect, and squeaked when John lifted it. But it worked. He rapped loudly at the door.

CHAPTER THREE

What answered him was silence; moreover, silence with an echo. I suppose there are few emptier sounds than that of knocking which goes on and on through a deserted house. And yet, somehow, there was the feeling that the place wasn't quite deserted; that someone—something—was still there, or had been until recently. The place itself, the cottage, the crowding trees, seemed to be listening.

"He's not there," said John at length, rather loudly.

"He must be." It was Margaret, now, who felt sure that the cottage was occupied. "He might just be scared to answer."

"But that's silly. Why should he be?"

"I would be, if I lived here, in the middle of

the wood, and someone came knocking just as the sun was going down."

"Well," retorted John, "but he's a grown man, and—"

"And I'm only a girl? Oh, sure! No, what I really meant was, he may not want to answer. He was crying, remember."

John hesitated. "Yes, I see what you mean. All right, we'll give him a minute to—well, to get hold of himself, then we'll try the back door. And if there's still no answer, we'll give up. Okay?"

"Okay."

There had once been a flagged pathway round the cottage, close to the wall, but this was now almost completely covered with flowering weeds, daisies, speedwells, tiny bellflowers, purple and blue and white. The creepers on the cottage walls—ivy mainly, and honeysuckle—were so thick and wild, and sagged so far from the wall in places, that the children had to leave the pathway and push through the thick tangle of bramble and fern that had overgrown the flower beds. Here and there tall spikes of foxgloves spired up into the sunshine. Butterflies moved sleepily over the blackberry flowers.

They trod carefully round to the back of the cottage. There had never been a garden here, only a little yard cleared from the forest growth, and floored with bricks beaten into the ground. These were now slippery with moss, and you could go on them as quietly as on a carpet. In the middle of the yard was a well. It had a low parapet of mossy bricks with a frame over it from which hung a rope with a wooden bucket attached.

The children paused by the well to look about them.

The back of the cottage was in fairly heavy shadow, but sunshine still lighted the porch roof, and the two windows, one to either side of the doorway. The windows had no glass in them, but there were wooden shutters folded back against the wall outside. These were unpainted, but looked clean, and the children could see into a corner of the nearer room, which was furnished after a fashion. There was a heavy chest against the wall and beside it a wooden stool. A crucifix hung on the wall above the chest.

Reassured by this, they approached the door. This was almost hidden under the weight of ivy sagging from the broken porch. John touched Margaret's arm, and pointed. It was just possible to see, behind the curtain of ivy, that the door stood open. And it gave straight into the back room of the cottage.

The porch was so small that both children could hardly crowd into it together. John knocked at the half-open door.

Again, there was no reply. They waited a little longer, then, very gently, John pushed at the door. It swung a little wider. They could see into the room.

It was obvious that this was the main living

and sleeping room of the house. There was a bed, with a tumble of blankets on it, a table, a big black cupboard in one corner, a wooden bench, a chair with a faded blue cushion on the seat, a couple of stools. A jug stood on the table, with a mug made of some dark metal, like pewter, and a wooden spoon. The fireplace held nothing but a pile of cold ashes. From a hook above it hung a black pot on a chain, like a cauldron.

No one was there, nobody at all. Just the same silence, and the swiftly deepening shadows of the forest at sunset.

"Well," said John aloud, cheerfully, and with a kind of relief, "that settles it. If he does live here, he's been home and gone out again. And if it's not his house—"

"Oh, but it is," said Margaret, in a queer voice. "Look. There, on the bed."

She pointed. There, among the pile of blankets, they could see it all quite clearly. Faded velvet, that even in this dim light showed scarlet; gilt buttons; a cloak of blue-grey with a hood; blue-grey hose, and a studded belt. And on the floor beside the bed, a pair of soft brown shoes with pine needles still clinging to the leather.

Without quite realizing what they did, both children had entered the cottage and stood staring down at the things on the bed. "The clothes he was wearing," said Margaret. "He came back here, changed his things, and then went out again. I knew they were fancy dress!"

"Well, that's fine," said John. He dropped the medallion on top of the clothes. It went with a clink and a shimmer. "There. We can just leave the thing here for him to find, and go straight back. We've been far longer than we meant to. Daddy's probably fuming—or else he's on the way to meet us."

The thought was somehow rather cheering. It was, indeed, suddenly quite dark. The sun had set with great rapidity, and the crowding trees did the rest. The air was still warm, but the silence of the forest was deeper than before. The insect hum had faded. No bird called.

Except the owl. One hooted, whisperingly far away among the pines. Then suddenly, another answered, from quite near at hand. Not the whispering *tuwhoo* this time, but the dreadful screech that goes by in the night like murder, leaving the small creatures crouching, terrified, in their hiding places.

"Your watch must have stopped! Come *on!*" cried Margaret, and, seizing John's hand, she pulled him towards the cottage door.

Then she screamed. John did not scream, but he made a sound like a shrill gasp with no breath in it. The two children, still holding hands, shrank backwards till they came right up against the bed.

In the cottage doorway, yellow eyes fixed and gleaming, jaws open and long tongue lolling, stood an enormous wolf.

CHAPTER FOUR

The children stood quite still, rooted with terror. The wolf lowered his head, and his upper lip lifted. The fangs were long and white, and showed glistening in the twilight. He made no sound, but his neck and back seemed to swell as the hair rose.

He was going to spring. His haunches gathered under him. His great muscles bunched.

The terrifying moment seemed to last for ever, but it can only have been a split second. Just before the wolf moved, John yelled—something half savage and half scared—grabbed the nearest thing to hand, and threw it. It was the heavy gold medallion. Only afterwards did they realize that, at the very moment when John

whirled the thing round his head like a chain
shot, the wolf had already turned to bolt. One
moment the door was blocked by his terrible
crouching shadow; the next, the doorway was
empty, and he was gone, like a ghost, into the
dusk of the forest. The chain and medallion
went whizzing after him. They heard the soft,
swift gallop of the wolf's retreat, the clink and
rustle as the medallion flew out of sight among
the brambles, then the stillness of the forest
came back, like someone shutting down a pad-
ded lid.

Margaret found that she could move. She ran
to the cottage door and shut it. There was a
thick wooden bar. She lifted this and slid it into
place, locking the door.

"Quick, John, the window! Pull the shutters
tight!"

"No good," said John. He sounded breathless,
as well he might, and also just a little bit pleased
with himself. Again, as well he might. "We can't
stay here. We'll have to chance it and go."

"But the wolf may come back. Or Daddy will
come for us. If we stay—"

"That's the point, don't you see? We can't let
him start down through the forest if he doesn't
know there really are wolves there. We didn't
believe it ourselves, in spite of its being called
Wolf Wood."

"The tracks," offered Margaret, without hope.
"He'd see them."

"We only saw them because we were follow-
ing the man, and it's dark now. Anyway, even

if he did see them, that wouldn't make him turn back. He'd come to get us, wouldn't he? Look, we can take something, a weapon or something, and we'll run the whole way. Besides—"

He stopped and his glance slid away from hers.

"What?" asked Margaret.

John said reluctantly: "Well, did you notice anything about the wolf?"

She hesitated, then he said it himself.

"I got the idea that it was scared."

Margaret nodded slowly. She knew that John would have liked to keep the credit for scaring the wolf away. That was only natural. But he had been brave, anyway, to stand up to it at all; and now, because he didn't like admitting that the wolf was scared, she could believe him. She said: "Well, I wouldn't have thought that if it had been starving, or terribly wild and savage, it would have run away just when a gold chain thing was chucked at it."

"No. But it was running already before I chucked it. You did see that? In fact, Meg, was it really a wolf? Maybe it was that man's dog?"

"Then it's a pretty rotten dog if it runs away from two children who've broken into its master's house. Tray wouldn't."

"Then it's a pretty rotten wolf, too," said John. "Whatever it is, I don't think it's terribly dangerous, and we'd be far better getting back to the car as quickly as we can, instead of waiting here. Let's get something a bit bigger to scare it with again, if it comes back." While he was talking he had been looking round for a weapon of some sort. Now he came up with a heavy stick which had been standing in the corner by the door. "Look, this'll do fine. If there's another one for you—"

"This'll be better," said Margaret, picking something up from among the discarded clothes on the bed. It gleamed in her hand. It was the long knife that the weeping man had been carrying. "It's funny he went out without it, but lucky for us."

She could see from John's face that he was wishing he had found the knife for himself. Her hand tightened round it. "No, you keep the stick. I like this better."

"You've never used a knife in your life."

"Nor have you, except to eat peas with."

They giggled, more with nerves than because they thought it was much of a joke. John gave a grunt. "Well, fair enough. It takes strength to bash with a cudgel—"

"But even a girl can stab with a knife?"

"You said it. Well, now or never. Let's go."

"What about the gold thing? It's somewhere out there in the brambles, and we'd never find it now, even if we dared look for it."

"We'll just have to tell Daddy about it, and come back with him tomorrow. We'll have to bring the knife and the stick back, anyway. And if that really was a wolf, someone in St. Johann will know about it, and Daddy will know what to do. Now come on. Go carefully till we see if the track is clear at the front of the cottage, then run like smoke."

They crept out of the doorway, leaving the door open as they had found it, and tiptoed to the corner of the cottage wall. John peered round. Nothing moved in the deep dusk of the forest. There was no sound. He took a fierce grip on the heavy-headed stick, and jerked his head to his sister. Quickly, but still stealthily, the children stole through the waist-high mass of fern and bramble, making for the crumbled wall that marked the garden's boundary. If nettles brushed them, they did not notice. The herbs crushed by their feet breathed a dozen sweet and spicy scents out into the cooling air. Moths, waking for the night, floated up from the disturbed leaves like feathers from a shaken pillow. Even the moss underfoot seemed to make a soft, spongy sound as they trod on it, so quiet was the forest.

Then they were scrambling across the broken wall, and under their feet was the smooth, pine-carpeted floor of the forest.

They ran.

Up the first slope, where the path was still faintly visible in the dusk. Into the twisting track, careful now of the tree roots that reached like webs for their feet, and the occasional trap of a fallen branch. Round the bend and along the level, with the great trees enormous in the dusk and windless air. The twilight smelled of resin, and rotting twigs, and of the scuffed pine needles as they ran. Now and again a small sound would raise the hairs on their necks; some twig, snapping of its own accord, would send down a spatter of needles, or a fistful of dead cones. The owl hooted again, not far away.

The forest was empty. No shadows moved. The track was empty, too. No Father came to meet them. They ran on.

Here at last was the fallen pine, and beyond it the track started its long slant uphill towards the road. It was fairly steep, but even if it had been pitched like a house roof I doubt if the children would have noticed, or slowed down for it. They had long ago stopped trying to run quietly; now, breathing hard, and no longer turning to look back, they pounded up the last long stretch. The trees retreated from the track's edge; there were open places, and foxgloves pale in the dusk, and the feathery shapes of fern. A wren, disturbed from sleep, flew up into a tree and scolded shrilly. The sound echoed through the forest like a fire alarm. It must be the same wren that had scolded them before. There, surely, just ahead, was the picnic place, and above it the main road where the car was parked.

They reached it and stopped, fighting for breath. They looked about them. Then looked again, bewildered. It was certainly the same place. There was the triangle of grass; there was the signpost; there was the tree stump where John had left the note, and the place where the rug had lain.

But no rug. No sign of Father. And, when they had run up to the road, no sign, either, of the car. Nothing.

They stood in the middle of the roadway and looked at one another. It was so dark now that hardly anything could be made out. The road itself showed only as a dim grey ribbon leading away over the brow of the hill. Down between the trees, in the valley bottom, where the castle stood, they thought they saw a light, dimly twinkling. But the place would be shut by now, and it was a very long way away. And they both knew how far it was back to their hotel. Against all belief, their parents had driven away and left them here alone, in the middle of this dark and deserted landscape.

Margaret was fighting off a strong desire to cry. All should have been well, now, but instead...Now she had time to realize how tired she felt, and how hungry. John, though he tried not to show it, felt the same cold and stunned dismay. The thing about being brave and reacting bravely to a strong crisis, like the appearance of the wolf, is that when it is over your whole mind and body seem to suffer a letdown. He felt hungry, too, and found that the hand that still gripped the knotted stick had begun to tremble just a little. When he spoke, he had to work hard to keep his voice cheerful, as an elder brother should.

"They must have thought we'd gone the other way. They've gone to look for us along the road. They'll be back soon."

"Perhaps this isn't the right place."

"Oh, it is. Wait a minute, look, isn't that my note still on the tree stump? Yes, well, that's what's happened; that's why they've gone off; he didn't see it. But I would have thought—oh, Meg, *look*!"

His tone changed completely. He bent to pick something up. Hidden under the ferns, where it must have spilled from the rug as Mr. Begbie lifted it, was a bar of chocolate; a big thick slab of milk chocolate packed solid with nuts and raisins.

"*That's* where it was! I thought we'd dropped it on the way down from the car! Boy, oh, boy! Here, halvers?"

He broke the slab in two, and handed one half to Margaret. Both children ate eagerly. They could hardly have found any food which would so quickly restore their strength and spirits. By one consent they each ate half of the piece they had, put the other half away in a pocket, then climbed to the road again to take a drink from the spring that bubbled in the bank above. Then, once more, they took stock. They stood still, listening for the sound of the returning car.

"Because," said John, "that's what'll happen. Daddy can't have seen that note, or he'd have picked it up. Perhaps they thought we'd gone along the road—been nervous of the forest, maybe. They'll drive along for a bit, and when they don't see us, they'll come back. In any case, the only sensible thing to do is to stay right here. Like being lost on a mountain or something...if you know people will come looking for you, stay where you are. They'll find us. And that was all rot about the wolves. I don't believe that creature was even a wolf at all. I think he was that chap's dog, a sort of Alsatian cross or something. Or else just a lost dog on the scrounge, and we scared him. There aren't wolves in the forest, how could there be? If we stay here, near the road, we'll be all right."

"And if they don't come back for us?"

"They're sure to, aren't they? For all we know, something's happened, like Mummy being taken ill, and Daddy having to drive her back to St. Johann without waiting for us. They'll come. And if they're not here by the time it's light, in the morning, we'll start walking back towards St. Johann. It's that way, and once we get to the main road, we'll get a lift or something."

"Couldn't we go now?" asked Margaret, with a half-glance behind her at the forest darkness.

"No," said John decidedly. "The best thing is to stay where you are. Besides, it isn't safe to stop cars at night and ask for lifts. We stay here. You'll see, they'll soon be back, and probably hopping mad with us, too."

"It wasn't our fault."

"I know, but they never stop to think of that. Well, they'll be here soon. I just wish they'd left the rug, but it's nice and warm, and there's no wind. Let's make a hollow in the ferns, and sit down."

The ferns were waist-high, and gave off a de-

licious scent when crushed. The children soon
had a soft, draft-proof nest, with their backs
against the tree stump. They settled there, talking a little at first, but in whispers, because the
night was so still.

Then after a while, because of that same unbroken stillness, they stopped talking, and sat
rather close to one another for comfort, listening
for the sound of the returning car.

CHAPTER FIVE

As soon as the horn woke the children, they knew what it was, though neither of them had ever heard a hunting horn before. The sound, high and silver and hollow as an echo, pierced the blue morning air and wound on over the hillsides and back into the valleys like the call of a herald wind.

They sat up in their nest of fern, still half asleep and stiff from the damps of dew, and, for a few bewildering moments while they rubbed the sleep from their eyes, not remembering anything about what had happened or where they were.

Then it all came back. The walk through Wolf

Wood, the cottage, the wolf-like beast, the disappearance of their father and mother and the car...

They jumped to their feet. Sure enough, it was morning. The sun was not yet up, but light was growing, sparkling back from the wet ferns, and drawing the dew upwards in curls of mist. And the car had not come back for them.

They were looking about them, wordlessly, in dismay, when they heard the horn again. This time it sounded much nearer. With it, apparently approaching fast along the road from the direction of St. Johann, came the flurry and thunder of galloping hoofs. A lot of them. A troop. The air was suddenly full of the music of bridles, and the sounds of shouting and laughter and view-hallooing, and the baying of hounds.

"A hunt!" cried John, seizing Margaret's hand. "Come on! There may be someone—"

He didn't finish. As they began to run up towards the road, something fled down and past them, and vanished into the forest. A wolf, or a creature like a wolf. They caught a glimpse of the wild, golden eyes, the grey pelt tagged with mud and damp, the long muzzle flecked with froth, and the lolling tongue. Then the creature was gone, and the hunt was almost on them.

The hounds first, a score of big dogs, as shaggy as the wolf itself, eyes and ears eager, for wolfhounds hunt by sight and not by scent. Where the track forked down from the road the pack faltered, paused, broke up and cast around, milling about among the trees at the forest's edge. There may have been danger to the children, but luckily there was no time to find out. As John and Margaret scrambled up onto the tree stump and waved, the first of the riders was there, cantering down among the hounds, to whip them back to the road. A dozen or so others checked their mounts on the road, waiting, while another man rode straight down the track and drew his big bay up with a slither of hoofs, just beside the children.

Margaret thought that he regarded them with a good deal of curiosity, but all he did was cry out: "Which way?" And, unbelievingly, she saw that his hand had gone to a pouch at his belt and pulled out a silver coin.

Beside her, she felt John draw breath to answer, but, without quite knowing why, she found herself leaning across him and pointing, not down towards the forest, where the wolf had gone, but up along the slope above the road, where the forest climbed away towards the hill-top.

"There! He went up there! Only a minute ago! Hurry!"

The man flicked the coin to her, wheeled his horse, and cantered back to the road. Whips cracked, men shouted, a woman's voice called something shrill and excited, and the hunt was off, the thunder of hoofs shaking the hillside.

The children got slowly down from the tree stump, and brushed the fern and grass from their clothes. Then, still without speaking, they

found the rest of the chocolate and began to eat
it. This time it did not lift their spirits quite as
it should have done. Munching it, they started
up the track to the roadway. Then stopped
where the signpost had stood. There was no
signpost. They looked, without surprise, at the
muddied roadway, marked and pitted by the
horses' hoofs. There was no sign of the familiar
tarmacadam road at all; no parking area; no
telegraph poles and wires; only a narrow dirt
road, like a farm track, beaten flat by hoofs.

"Of course, it's a dream," said Margaret. The
thought seemed to cheer her. Dreams were
things that couldn't harm you, and that came
to an end.

"Of course." John chewed chocolate for a minute, thinking hard. "I suppose you noticed how
those people were dressed?"

"Yes. Like *Richard the Second,* when the
school party saw it at Stratford."

"Mm." John swallowed chocolate. "Or like the
people in that story I was reading, about the
Hundred Years' War. I was telling you about
it; it was pretty exciting. That's what's happened. I've been reading too much, so I'm having
this dream."

"Well, so am I," said Margaret, rather sharply.
"It's *my* dream, and you're a part of it."

"I feel as if it's *my* dream, and *you're* a part
of it."

"I—I suppose it must be a dream?" faltered
Margaret.

"What else? There was a good tarmac road

here yesterday, and it's gone. And look, so has the note I left for Daddy! The chocolate's the only thing— Hey, Meg!"

"What?"

"That coin he threw you, just as if he was a duke or something, and you were a poor peasant girl...you put it in your pocket. Let's see."

She pulled it out, and they looked at it. It was familiar. There was the head of the monarch, crowned. Above it was his name: OTHO DUX.

"Just like the medallion!" exclaimed Margaret.

"Except that the man's older," said John. "And look, it says OTHO DUX this time. Duke, I suppose? Well, that's heads. Now for tails." He turned the coin over.

Margaret peered over his shoulder. "It's different. There was that Latin word on the other. 'Faithful,' you said it meant. This has just got a bird or something. What is it, John, an eagle?"

"Something like that. But look, it's got a date."

They looked at the date in silence: 1342.

"And the coin's new," said John at length.

"So was the medallion."

"Gold always looks new. Anyway, the medallion's got to be older than this. The man— Duke Otho—was young then, and maybe he wasn't Duke yet, either. But you can bet he is now. This coin's hardly been used. Well, it goes with the clothes, doesn't it? And the horses, with all the coloured harness, and bells, and those huge wide stirrups, and the awful spurs."

"And the lady. Did you see her? Sidesaddle, in green velvet, with a cloak."

"Here," he said, "put it away again. Pity it's just a dream coin, it's probably valuable. Thirteen forty-two...I wish I could remember any history at all! It's the Middle Ages, that's all I know. And we're still in the same country as we were last night, and it does look pretty much the same—"

"Except for the road, and the telegraph poles—"

"And the signpost, and look, there are lots more trees, and there's more forest right down into the valley instead of fields, and—"

"The castle!" cried Margaret. It was hidden from where they stood by a thicket of bushes. "Don't you remember? When we went round it with Daddy they said it was fourteenth century—oh, fourteenth. Then that's no good."

"Yes, it is. Thirteen forty-two *is* fourteenth century, same as 1980 is twentieth. What do you bet it's still there, and brand-new, with all flags flying? Come on!"

They ran back to the tree stump. There below them, between the tree trunks, was the castle on its hill, walls and towers and moat and bridge, with the river running a little way beyond. But it was no brand-new fourteenth-century castle. It was still a ruin, and the moat was still dry.

For all that, there were differences. The road leading to the bridge, where Daddy had driven them yesterday, was a mere track, no wider than the one where they stood. The bridge, even, was broken; halfway across the reeds and mud of the moat it had collapsed into a welter of rotten timber. There was no sign of the hut where they had bought tickets; no sign of the cottages beside the meadow where they had parked the car.

They stared at the scene in the silence of dismay. At length John put it into words. "No castle, no car park. No cottages, and the new bridge is broken. Looks as if it's not the Middle Ages after all! And yet it's not our own century.... The whole thing's crazy!"

"Yes, and another thing," said Margaret slowly. "That man who asked which way the wolf had gone. He wasn't speaking German, was he? And *I* certainly can't! But we are still in the same place. It *must* still be Germany, even if it's a different century. But it did sound like English to me, and I could understand what the other people were saying to each other, too. It *was* English, wasn't it? But why?"

"Dream language, that's why!" said John firmly though he understood no more than his sister. "Ever had a dream about landing on a strange planet, or talking to animals, or something? I'll bet if you dreamed about ancient Rome *they'd* be talking English, too! The main thing is, we *can* talk to them."

"Well, all right, but what do we do now?"

"It doesn't seem to matter much," said John, with a bravado he didn't really feel, "since it's only a dream. But one thing's for sure, no car's ever coming down *that* beastly little road! What's more, we don't even know if St. Johann's still there so it's no good starting to walk. And dream or no dream, I'm hungry. At least we've got some money to buy food with, and we'll know how to ask for it. So there's only one thing we *can* do that makes sense."

"Go back to the cottage, and ask the man to help us?"

"That's it. If it's there."

Margaret gasped, then said firmly: "It'll be there. The castle's still there, after all, even if it doesn't fit into one world or the other. And when we saw the cottage yesterday it did look as if it had been there, just the same, for hundreds of years."

"Yesterday?" said John.

She caught her breath again. "You mean that was a dream, too? Before we went to sleep? But I remember it quite distinctly, don't you?"

"If we're both still asleep on the rug beside Daddy, then it *was* a dream, and the wolf and everything. And if we're dreaming, then we can't come to harm, can we? We might as well pass the time somehow! And I really am hungry. There must be something to eat in that cottage, whether he's there or not."

"If he is, we can tell him where the medallion went."

"And give him back his knife and stick," said John. "We've still got those, so I'll bet the cottage is still there. Yesterday must have been part of the same dream."

"So was the wolf," said Margaret. "Oh, yes, it's the same dream. He'll be there, and the wolf will be somewhere, too. It went that way."

There was a pause. "I don't see what else to do," said John at length. "Wait here for the hunt to come back?"

"Having found that I sent them the wrong way? Not likely! Let's go to the cottage. I liked the weeping man better than those people on horseback, somehow. Here, do you want the knife this time?"

But John kept to his stick. They started down the track. The sound of the hunt had long since gone. The forest was as silent as before. It was not as frightening as it had been last night in the dusk, but they hurried, keeping rather close together, and watching all the time for movement among the crowding columns of the trees.

"Why did you send them the wrong way?" asked John.

"Why do you think?"

"It *was* a wolf, you know."

"So what?" retorted Margaret. "If it was the same wolf, and I'm sure it was, then it hadn't hurt us. And did you see its eyes?"

John said nothing. He had seen its eyes. The children walked on in silence after that, each wondering what they would do if the cottage was not there, each convincing themselves that they were dreaming, because this was the only comfort and safeguard they could think of in a rather scary situation. Each, in consequence, was sure that the other was only a person in a dream, and therefore unreal, and unlikely to be of help if any danger came. It was not a comforting idea. It lasted them all the way to the cottage.

For the cottage, after all, was there. And not, as Margaret half expected, newly built and with its garden tidy and well planted; like the castle, it looked pretty well the same as it had done yesterday. This time they did not trouble to knock at the front door. They walked round to the back, which they had left open in their hasty flight.

It was shut.

Three seconds later both children were at the window, peering cautiously into the room. This was just the same as yesterday, but for one thing. The tumbled clothes had gone from the bed, and were flung over a chair. In the bed was a man, asleep. He was lying facing the window, and they could see him clearly. It was the weeping man of Wolf Wood.

He opened his eyes, and saw them.

CHAPTER SIX

Half an hour later the children were sitting at
the table in the cottage living room, finishing
a strange but satisfying breakfast. The bread
was dark and coarse, and rather dry, and there
was no butter, but there was a strong, tangy
piece of honeycomb on a wooden dish, and a
bowl of the most delicious wild strawberries.
The fire was burning merrily, and the room
looked as different from yesterday as a new nest
does from a last year's one. Their host, shaved
and dressed, sat on a settle near the fire. He
would not take breakfast, but had drawn a cup
of ale from a barrel in the corner. The children
had tumblers (which their host called goblets)

of some strong, sweet drink tasting rather like honey.

To their relief, the "dream language" worked here, too. At first, when the sleeping man had opened his eyes and seen them peering in at him through the window, they had been nervous, and half inclined to run away yet again. But instead of looking annoyed at being spied on, he had seemed glad to see them. He waved to them to stay where they were, and in a moment or two came quickly out of the cottage, wrapped in his grey cloak, and, before they had time to say much more than a shy "Good morning," he had invited them in and found food for them, "and fire to dry your clothes, for there is danger," he said gently, "in the damps of the nighttime forest."

So they ate and drank while he drew water from the well outside, and went into the inner room to wash and dress himself. Then, as he sat with his ale, they told him their story, which, said John, hesitating, was "only a dream, really. That is, if you don't mind being just someone in someone's dream? Because it *must* be a dream, Mummy and Daddy vanishing like that, and the road and the signpost, and then all this is so queer, this place, and—" He stopped. He had been going to say "your clothes, and the way you talk," but that sounded rude, so he finished, a bit lamely, "those people who were hunting the wolf."

"I do not disdain to be part of your dream," said the man. "In fact, in a moment I shall tell

you why I am glad of it. But part, at least, of
your tale is no dream to me. When I first saw
you, out there by the window, you were bearing
my knotted staff, and the little maid, Margaret,
had—if I mistook it or not—my own hunting
knife in her hand."

Margaret felt herself blushing. She had put
the knife down quickly on the table as she followed her host into the cottage, and she had
seen John restoring the stick to its place with
the same secretive haste. "Yes, I had," she con-
fessed. "But after we'd seen the wolf we were
scared of going back through the wood without
any sort of weapon, so we borrowed them. We
really did mean to bring them back. We would
have come down again with Daddy, and brought
them. In any case we'd have had to come back
to tell you where we found the amulet, and how
we'd thrown it away again, at the wolf."

For that it was an amulet, and not merely a
medallion, their host had explained to them
almost straight away. One of the first things
they had noticed, when he came back, fully
dressed, from the inner room, was that he had
the gold chain and amulet round his neck. He
had found it, he said briefly, among the brambles. Its value to him, he told them, was as a
talisman, or amulet against evil; he said nothing about its being gold, though the children
were now convinced that it was. When they told
him how they had found it beside the fallen tree,
he merely thanked them for bringing it to the

cottage, nor did he seem angry that John had
thrown it away again at the wolf.

Now, as Margaret spoke, he smiled. It was
amazing how the smile changed him. When
they had first seen his face, distorted as it had
been by grief, it had still been a good face, a
face with, even, something noble about it in the
strongly marked brows and the pleasant mouth
and the longish, high-bridged nose. Now, as he
smiled at them, the lines of grief still showed,
and the impression that something terrible had
been endured in the recent past, but his eyes
were kind, and about him there was a sort of
eagerness and hope that had surely not been
there before.

"I never doubted you, little maiden. You were
welcome to anything that my poor cottage could
afford you. I am only sorry that the wolf frightened you so. Yet, you tell me, you turned the
Duke's hunt away from his trail, and sent them
coursing away through the upper forest. Why
did you do that?"

"Because I hate hunts," said Margaret. "And
the wolf hadn't hurt us. In fact we both thought
he was scared of us himself. Have you seen him?
Is he really a wolf? Is he tame?"

The man shook his head. "No. He is wild indeed, a fierce wolf of the forest—but only in
darkness. When you saw him first, at the cottage door, the darkness had barely begun to fall.
It was the half-light, the owl-light, when the
hour hangs, as they say, between the wolf and
the dog."

The children looked at him curiously. "What do you mean?" asked John.

"He was still tame enough—dog enough—to be afraid of hurting you. But he knew that, in a few minutes' time, when darkness came fully, he would not be able to help himself, and would attack you. So he fled, even before you picked up the amulet to throw at him."

"I see. I thought the amulet must be magic, or something. I couldn't imagine a real wolf running away from it otherwise."

"Perhaps it is. I told you that I held it as a talisman against evil."

John finished his last slice of bread, drained his goblet, and wiped his mouth. He had noticed that their host wiped his mouth, very neatly, with the back of his hand, so apparently it was the thing to do. "You said you were going to tell us about that. How *did* you find it?"

"It was certainly no easy task." Their host regarded his hands rather ruefully. They were long and fine, but showed the marks of recent scratches. "It was deep among the thorns and nettles, and took me quite a time, even though I saw where it fell. It was the first thing I did when I got back here, to go and look for it. I knew that I would not be able to sleep until I had it safely once again."

"But—"

"Yes, but how did you *know?*"

Both children spoke at once, then were silent. Margaret had not meant her question to sound so abrupt, and found herself flushing. The man's eyes came to her, quickly.

"Yes?" he prompted gently.

Margaret swallowed. "I'm sorry, but I don't understand. How did you know the medallion—the amulet, I mean—fell in the brambles? You lost it up in the forest at the fallen tree. But you went and looked for it before we told you about the wolf, or anything. And you just said you *saw* where it fell. How?"

"Do you mean," asked John, "that you were here when the wolf came?"

"Yes." He regarded them as he spoke with a grave, sad look that held a touch of shame. Then he looked down at his hands again. There was a pause. Neither of the children could have spoken. Somehow, they no longer felt any surprise. But what he said next was the strangest of all the strange things that had happened:

"I was here, and you saw me. You see, I am the wolf."

A dream, thought Margaret, it is a dream. And of course, if I am dreaming, it's quite obvious that the weeping man is the same creature as the wolf of the wood. That could even be why he was weeping, because he knew the day was almost over and he must go back to his lair—his cottage—and take off his man's clothes, and run out, like a slavering beast, into the darkness to hunt and to kill. She shivered. They had come to that lair, she and John, at twilight, just as the strange and awful transformation had taken place. The man-wolf—"werwolf" was the word, she remembered—must have still been lurking nearby, and had heard them. Perhaps he had thought they were thieves. He had come snarling to the cottage door, but seen only a couple of children; seen, too, that the precious amulet (which he must have missed when he undressed) had been returned to him, and checked himself on the very verge of springing at them. Even with the darkness falling, even through the hooting of the owl, he had managed to control the savagery of his wolf's nature, and to force himself to run from the children before he harmed them.

When they saw him again, at daybreak, he was fleeing in desperation from the hunt to get back to his cottage before the daylight change overtook him. Once there, and a man again, he had plunged into bed, and the sleep of exhaustion. If she had not sent the hunt the wrong way, they might well have caught and killed him while he was still a wolf. They would not, as she had done without realizing it, have seen something human and familiar in the creature's wild, yellow eyes.

They were certainly the same eyes. She could see it now, quite clearly, though the man's eyes were not quite the same clear yellow as the wolf's, but a light, golden brown with hazel lights in them: good eyes. His hair was dark and long and carefully dressed, his skin smooth and well barbered, and his hands, though roughened with peasant's work, were smooth

and finely shaped, not hairy a bit, and the nails
were short…

She glanced up, saw him watching her, and
went scarlet.

He laughed. "And my teeth are not wolves'
teeth, either," he said.

"I didn't—I wasn't—" she stammered.

"Little maid," he said, "it would amaze me
not at all were you to run screaming from my
cottage! But you are brave, and you have noble
manners, and indeed, it would ill become me to
hurt you, wolf or man, when I owe my life to
you, and hope to owe you how much more."

He leaned forward and put another log on the
fire. "You are dry now, and you have eaten and
drunk enough? Then be comfortable, because it
is time I told you my story."

CHAPTER SEVEN

My name [said the werwolf] is Mardian, and once I was the servant and friend of the Duke whose men you saw hunting me today. He is Duke Otho, the ruler of this country, who holds the castle that lies beyond the forest's edge. My father was chief counsellor to Otho's father, Duke Hildebrand, and fought at his right hand in time of war. Otho and I were brought up together, and grew up as companions and close friends, sharing everything, pleasure and punishments alike. When the old Duke died, my father followed him within the week; and so Otho and I hoped to do also when our time came. You would smile were I to tell you of the vows we took as boys, of the blood-mingling and the long midnight talks...and how the amulet that you have seen became the symbol of the faith and trust we had vowed to one another.

I shall tell you [he went on] how this came about.

When Otho and I were first come to manhood at fifteen, we exchanged tokens. There was a goldsmith at the castle—he is dead now—whose work was famous. We had him make us two amulets of gold, as like as two peas, save that on one was the portrait of Otho, and on the other my own. Then we exchanged them, with vows I shall not tell you of, boys' vows and men's. It is enough now to say that the trust between us was kept unbroken, and that when Otho became Duke of the realm, I was at his right hand, and of all who surrounded him at his court, there was no man he would sooner trust with his life and all his secrets than me, Mardian.

Then, after a few years, a terrible thing happened. One day a raiding party, led by a certain count who was no friend of my master's, came riding straight across the Duke's land, and fell in with Otho himself, who was out hunting. There was a skirmish, well-armed troopers against lordlings attired for the hunt and lightly armed, and in the fighting Duke Otho was wounded. The raiders drew off at that, the affair having gone further than the Count, even in his malice, intended. But the Duke, in falling from his horse, caught his spur in the stirrup, and, the charger being hurt and bolting, was dragged some way before I could stop his horse and raise him. He recovered, but from that day to this he has been lame, and sits in his chair, or in a chair carried here and there by his servants.

That was five years ago. It followed that in matters of war—such as the expedition to punish Count Sigismund—I had to lead the soldiers; and in every other matter that needed a sound body. And you may guess what happened. The Duke's young son, Crispin, who was not yet ten years old at the time of the accident, grew towards manhood hardly remembering his father's prowess as a soldier and man of action, but looking more and more to me, Mardian, as a hero to follow and admire. To a young boy, the Duke to whom men turned for wisdom and judgment was of small account beside a fighting man. I had to train him, because men must fight and dukes must lead them, but always I strove to keep Duke Otho first in his love.

For a time all went well enough. Then came another tragedy. The Duchess, Otho's lady wife, fell sick and died. This happened when Prince Crispin was twelve years old. After this it could be seen that the Duke grew paler and more silent, and sometimes—when he was most in pain—short-tempered, and angry at small frets. He spoke harshly on occasions even to me, and showed scant patience with the prince. When I talked with the boy and tried to make him understand, Duke Otho grew angry again, and charged me with stealing his son's love.

Then one day, when in his pain and bitterness

he accused me of this, and even of wanting to usurp his dukedom, he was overheard by a courtier who himself nursed that very ambition. This was a man called Almeric, whom I had already suspected of plotting against the Duke's life and against the right of the young prince to succeed him.

At first Almeric, believing that I must have begun to hate the master who spoke so harshly to me, tried to tempt me from my allegiance with the prospect of power and gain. When he saw that I was faithful, he grew afraid that I would report to the Duke what had passed. So he tried to have me killed, first by poison, and when that failed, by the dagger in the dark. When that, too, failed, Almeric turned to sorcery.

I do not want to weary you, or to frighten you, with the tale of how the spell was cast, but for a year and more I have been as I am now. By day I am still Mardian, but the night, as you have seen, forces the wolf-shape on me, and with it the wolf's appetite and lust for blood. With sunrise the bloodlust goes, and my man's shape and mind return, but the memories and the shame remain.

Each night I, the wolf, go to the castle, to watch there for my enemy, but he is too wary to venture out. I wait till dawn—sometimes dangerously overlong—in the frail hope that my lord the Duke will come out to see the hunt. Each day, in the grey hours between dawn and sunrise, while I still loiter in wolf's form, they

come as you saw them, in winter and summer
alike, and they try to kill me. Almeric has offered a rich reward for the head of the "great
wolf," but he himself dare not ride out with the
hunt. He knows that, if I were to see him, I
would drag him from his horse and kill him,
though the hounds tore me to pieces the next
moment.

When I first suffered enchantment I fled to
this cottage. Here, years ago, an old woman
lived who had been nurse to some of the children
of the castle, among them Otho and myself. She
was a good soul, a wisewoman, and a healer;
but simple folk are ignorant, and took her for
a witch. She died years back, but even so no
villager would venture here, or even into this
part of the forest. So no one sees the working
of the dreadful spell that binds me. Here I am
safe.

But here, too, I have been trapped, waiting
through all these long months for a chance to
break the spell. A chance that may have come,
at last, through you.

Here Mardian fell silent, sitting with bowed
head, staring at the fire. The flames were dying
down now, but the room grew warm as the
morning sun rose higher.

He sat for so long that the children ventured
at length to speak. His last sentence had startled them considerably, and excited them, too.
Questions were buzzing in their minds.

"But why can't you just go to him yourself?"

asked Margaret. "In daylight, I mean, when you aren't a wolf? You could tell him everything, just as you're telling us—"

"And he'd believe you," put in John eagerly. "If he saw the spell working, he'd have to, wouldn't he?" He hesitated. "Hasn't he sent search parties out? I'd have thought that *soldiers* would have to go anywhere, even into a witch's wood, if they were told to! Or—" He stopped.

"Or?" prompted Mardian gently.

"Or does he think you left him of your own accord? Do you mean he hasn't even *tried* to get you back?"

"But even if you quarrelled," began Margaret hotly, "he ought to know—"

"There was no quarrel," said Mardian quickly. "You must not blame Duke Otho. He has not searched for me because he has not even missed me." He paused, nodding. "Yes, you may well look amazed. But my story is not yet done. I have not yet told you of the strangest and most terrible enchantment of all. The wicked Almeric has taken my form and appearance, and lives at the castle as 'Lord Mardian.'"

They stared.

"People think he's you?" This was Margaret. And from John:

"You mean he looks just like you?"

"Exactly like. To all appearances 'Mardian' has never left the castle. I know all this, because sometimes I travel, in disguise, to a village beyond the forest's edge to get food, and I listen in the marketplace for news. Almeric has no amulet, of course, but he has told Duke Otho that it is lost, and the Duke accepts this. Why should he not? He does not suspect a spell."

"But if you *did* go to him and showed him the amulet?" insisted Margaret.

"If he saw both of you together, he'd *know* it was a spell, and that you were the right one!" cried John.

Mardian smiled at the eager way in which they took his part, but it was a rueful smile. "Alas, I cannot hope even to enter the castle. I am told that all comers are stopped in the outer barbican by 'Mardian's' soldiers and put to question. I would be recognized, and killed, and the amulet taken from me. Or I would be shut in the dungeon and shown only after dusk—and then you know what they would do to the wild grey wolf who was locked in their trap! The Duke himself, were he to see me then, would raise no finger to stop them."

"Then how do you think—?" John cleared his throat and tried again. "You said that perhaps the time had come for the spell to be broken?"

"It is more than time," said Mardian strongly. "For the Duke's sake, and for the sake of the realm, the attempt must be made very soon." He straightened in his chair, his strange eyes fixed on the children, and glowing almost like a wolf's eyes. "I have heard other things in the marketplace. The Duke never leaves the castle now, and men fear that his health is failing, though his physicians can find no cause. It is said, too, that 'Mardian's' power grows, and that he keeps Prince Crispin with him constantly, as if he is indeed winning him away from his father. I believe that if the Duke dies soon—by enchantment or through some other means— then Crispin himself would only be allowed to live long enough to bequeath the dukedom to Almeric. After that he, too, would die."

"And the Duke really thinks that it's *you* doing all this?" cried Margaret.

"What else is he to think? He believes his eyes. Is it any wonder that, as I heard, he has torn his own amulet from his neck, and locked it away out of sight?"

John found that his heart was thumping hard. It all came back to the amulet, the golden token that had brought them to the cottage and into this strange and disturbing dream. He moistened his lips. "And since *you* can't get near the Duke, someone else has to try? With the amulet? Did you mean that it *is* magical?"

Mardian looked from one to the other of them. His look was so sad and worn that Margaret drew breath, impulsively, to say that they would do anything, anything...but John touched her arm, and she was silent. They waited, the only sound the rustle of the dying fire.

Mardian did not answer John's question directly. He glanced round him at the humble cottage room, then spoke, slowly, to the fire.

"When Otho and I were children, no older than you are now, the wisewoman told us, in this very room, that for every evil spell there is a remedy, and that for all evil there is good in the other arm of the balance. I have come to believe through these dark days that these two amulets, cast in love and faith and vows of honour, may hold some power that may be the answer to Almeric's wickedness. Power there certainly must be. When the enchanter drugged me, ready to cast his spell, he stripped my body of all my clothing. Yet when he drove me out into the forest to suffer the life of a werwolf, I found that the amulet was still round my neck."

He paused. Through the open door of the cottage came, startlingly beautiful in the silence, the rich fluting of a blackbird's song. As if it had been a signal, the werwolf raised his head and spoke to them straightly.

"You ask if there is magic to help you against magic. I do not know. I only know that in one short month Prince Crispin will be fifteen, and that his father the Duke will be dead. And in this time of need you have come to me. You are young, no more than children, but you had the courage to face the great wolf, and later you saved him from his killers, for no other reason than that you saw his frightened eyes. And you were brought to my door by the amulet. This is why I, Mardian, am content to put my fate, and so much more, into your hands."

John and Margaret looked at one another, not quite knowing what to say, but Mardian lifted a hand, and got to his feet. "No, say nothing yet. I am going out now, to walk in the forest, and leave you to talk between yourselves. What I

have asked you to do will not be easy and may
indeed prove perilous. But I will not use per-
suasion. You must decide freely, and for that I
will leave you alone." He stopped in the sunlit
doorway, looking back. "I shall come back at
midday, when the sun stands over the clearing.
If you decide to help me you will still be here.
If not, go with my blessing, but be sure to get
clear of the forest before dusk, or I may not be
able to answer for myself again."

Go? Where to? The children did not say it
aloud, but the werwolf smiled.

"Don't be afraid that you will not find your
way home. I believe that, if you do not vow yourselves to me, you will come safely out of the
spell before morning. For spell it is," he added
with a look of pity, "and no dream, my dears,
as you had hoped. This is real, as your own time
is real, and there is suffering to be won or to be
escaped from. It is for you to choose. Choice is
man's right, and for that I leave you free."

He turned and went out into the sunlight,
leaving the children to themselves.

You may imagine the discussion that followed. I do not think that John and Margaret
were any braver or better than most children.
Besides, in spite of what Mardian had said, they
tended still to think that such a strange expe-
rience could only be a dream, and so there could
be no real danger to them, whatever they un-
dertook to do. It was a storybook adventure, no
more, and they would waken from it the mo-

ment danger threatened, to find themselves safely back in their own familiar world. And, like any other children who read a lot of stories, they believed that this one must end happily, that with faith and courage and the right actions, everything would come out right in the end. Besides this, the glimpse they had had of the courtiers, and the prospect of actually seeing and living in a court such as they had read of many times, was very exciting. Danger was hardly to be believed in; the adventure was the thing.

So they spent hardly any time at all in arguing whether or not they should help the werwolf. It did not occur to them to refuse. They knew that if you find some person or creature in desperate need of help which you can supply, you have a human duty to supply it, even if it could inconvenience or even hurt you to do so. This, after all, is how the greatest and best deeds in the world have been done, and though the children did not say this aloud, they knew it inside themselves without even thinking about it.

What they really argued about, and were still arguing about when the werwolf came back at noon, was exactly what he would want them to do.

It sounded simple enough. "Almeric cannot suspect two children of anything, least of all of plotting with me," said Mardian. "Though he himself is an enchanter, he will not be expecting another spell to be working against him. He

cannot know that you would dare to walk into
Wolf Wood, so he will not think you dangerous.
Let us hope he will not even notice you. I must
not enter the castle, but I can show you how you
may go in and mix with the people there, until
you can come near enough to Duke Otho to have
a private word with him." He looked at John.
"Sooner or later, if you mix with the other boys,
you will be called on like his other pages to do
him some kind of service. When that happens,
as it surely must, then you must show him the
amulet, and tell him my story. Above all, let no
one but he touch it, or even see it. Put it straight
into his hand. He will remember the vows we
made, and know that the amulet is a call from
me for his help and trust. After that, it is with
him. He will know how to deal with Almeric.
Cripple or no, he is not Duke for nothing."

He slipped the amulet from his neck, and
handed it to John. The boy received it gingerly,
almost as if he feared it might burn him. He
looked doubtfully at the werwolf. "But what if
he simply doesn't believe me? What if he thinks
we just found the thing, and have come for a
reward or something?"

"Then hope is done. If trust dies, and vows
come to count for nothing, then I must stay a
forest wolf till they hunt me down to death.
There will be no more reason for me to stay a
man," said the werwolf.

CHAPTER EIGHT

The decision once taken, it was as if a load had been lifted from all of them: from the children, because somehow they knew this was what they ought to do—"what the enchantment happened for," as Margaret put it—and from the werwolf, because he was sure that the children's coming meant that the time was near for the breaking of the spell.

"How do we get into the castle?" asked John. "If everyone is stopped and searched—"

"There's a secret way. I shall show you the way in myself. It leads to a secret room that no one knows of except myself and the Duke. We used it as boys, but have not been there for many

years. You will not be found there. I shall take
you there at night, so that you can wait and
hide until morning, then, when you hear the
castle waking up, you must watch your chance
to slip out and mingle with the other young-
sters. Take time, and have patience, and you
will soon learn the way of things. And in time
you may be sure that your chance will come to
approach the Duke."

"'In time,'" repeated John. "I know, but
what's bothering me is, what will our parents
say? We've already been away all night—"

"No," said Mardian. "Time is not the same.
You will find, when you get home, that they
will not even have missed you. So forget your
own concerns, of your charity, and let us make
our plans, for time here is growing short."

John nodded. It seemed reasonable. In fact
both he and Margaret were already finding it
hard to remember what "home" and "the holi-
day" had been like. Already they seemed to belong to this strange, rather alarming, remote
and magic age where dukes ruled in lonely cas-
tles, and evil men ambitious of power stole a
good man's life and happiness and condemned
him to a long prison. They were too young to
know that every age is the same, for men do not
alter. But the trappings alter, and it must be
admitted that the two of them thoroughly en-
joyed trying on and choosing the clothes that
their host produced from the chest in the other
room.

"There should be some garments here to fit

you," he said. "Old Gulda spent all her time mending and making for the children. Many a time she saved Otho and me a whipping, and made our torn hose as good as new after some escapade. Here, little maid, try these."

It was like the best kind of dressing-up. The clothes were real ones, not makeshifts or stage clothes; the belts were real soft calfskin and the buckles were silver-gilt studded with stones— turquoises for John, garnets for Margaret. Most of the garments were worn, and mended here and there, because, with everything handwoven and handmade, as Mardian explained, they had to last for many years. Certainly, when at last they were dressed to their satisfaction, both children looked as if the clothes had belonged to them for a long time.

There was a mirror, speckled and dim with disuse like everything else in the room. It seemed to be made of metal, and was spotted with rust. They studied themselves.

John wore hose—tights—in thick wool the colour of ivy leaves, and a dark-blue woollen tunic. He had rather hankered for a bright one of robin red, but the werwolf had shaken his head.

"It were best," he said, "to keep to the dark colours, and the greys. There may be need to hide, and to go softly in darkness."

So Margaret was in a grey dress which came down almost to her ankles, with a full skirt and long close-fitting sleeves. Over it went a loose, sleeveless garment of deep reddish brown; Mardian called this a surcoat, and said that the colour was "murrey." She carried a little purse of stitched leather at her belt, with her handkerchief and the silver piece that the huntsman had thrown to her. Both children found shoes that fitted easily, a kind of ankle-boot with pointed toes, of skin as soft as washleather. What pleased John perhaps most about his costume was that from his belt was hung a hunting knife something like the one that Mardian wore. It was thrust through the straps of his leather pouch. Its hilt, like the belt and pouch, was set with turquoises, and it was very sharp.

"I'll have to watch not to cut my mouth," he said, feeling it. Then he looked up, wide-eyed, at the werwolf. "I knew—I didn't know—how did I know that?" he stammered, then said wonderingly: "Do I really use this knife for eating?"

Mardian nodded. "Yes. Do you not do so in your home and in your own time?"

John knitted his brows, trying to remember. "Well, yes, in a way, but not like this. But I do know how you do it. Does this really mean that we, well, that we sort of belong here?"

"I think so. I think that already you are part of this world. You will not feel strange. Has it not struck you with wonder that you and I already talk the same language, yet you told me that you had come from a land across the sea, and knew nothing of the language of this country?"

"We'd already wondered about that," said

John, "then we decided we were dreaming. It sounds just like English to us."

"*Aren't* you talking English, Mr.—Lord Mardian?" asked Margaret.

"I think," said their host, "that you had better not call me Mardian. You will have to keep that for the false Lord Mardian, and you must make no mistake. Call me Wolf. It's a good enough name, and an easy one. No, little maid, I do not speak 'English.' And to me your name sounds like 'Gretta,' and John's is 'Hans.' Now listen. If anyone asks you who you are, tell them this, and say that you are the grandchildren of the Lady Grisel. She is very old, and has long since lost count of all her descendants. Besides, her mind wanders now, and she lives in a world where past and present are confused and dim. Even if she says she does not know you, no one will doubt you. For the rest, your parents are dead, and you are wards of Duke Otho. This means that if any suspicion falls on you, you will be taken to the Duke, which is what we want. But I doubt if anyone will suspect you at all. Now, little Gretta, if you should be questioned, what will you say?"

Quite without thinking about it, Margaret found herself dropping a little curtsy, her grey skirts held wide. "So please you, sir, we are Hans and Gretta, wards of the Duke himself, and the Lady Grisel is our grand-dame."

The werwolf was smiling. "You see? You need have no fear that those in the castle will think you strange. Now, Hans, take the amulet and put it in your pouch, and keep it close. Then we must talk, and quickly. See, the afternoon is drawing on already, and once the sun sets, you know that I shall be able to tell you nothing more. Come, let us go back to the other room, and you shall eat and drink again, and we will make our plans."

They followed him into the outer room. "Wolf," began Margaret, then stopped.

"What troubles you, little maid?"

She hesitated, then said in a rush: "I don't want to hurt your feelings, but you did say you were going to take us after dark to the castle, and show us the secret room. Well, if you're— I mean, if you change—"

"If I am a wolf after dark, how can you come near me without danger?"

"Yes," said Margaret, miserably.

He looked down at her for a moment with those sad eyes, then turned away to the window. He spoke with his back to the children. "Because as soon as the twilight falls I shall go out into the forest, in my beast form, and kill, and eat my fill. After that—only after that—I can count myself safe. You will be able to trust me until morning."

"Oh, but we do trust you—" began John.

The werwolf turned quickly. "Do not do so! Wait until I have been out, and come again." He added strongly: "As soon as the sun sets you must go into the inner room there, and lock the door and put some heavy barrier—the clothes-chest—against it. Whatever you hear, do not open the door. I cannot answer for myself. Please believe me. And close the shutter on the window, and drop the bar. *Do not open the door.* I shall come back after the moon has risen, when all is safe. When you see moonlight through the shutters, open them and watch for me. Do you understand?"

"Yes. We promise," said John.

"But there's something I don't understand," put in Margaret. "Won't it be awfully dangerous—for you, I mean—to go up to the castle with us?"

"As dangerous as any other night, but there is no choice, since we cannot go by daylight. You could not find the way into the secret chamber without me. Nor can I, in my wolf-form, open windows and doors to go in myself. So we go at night, together. Now—" this with a quick glance at the sky outside, "I must tell you how we will enter the castle. See, I have made a drawing of it, and here, near the drawbridge, is the window where once Otho and I pulled out the bars and made a private way...."

As the sun dropped at last below the tops of the trees, the werwolf rose, folded the parchment, and put it away on the shelf in the corner cupboard. During the warmth of the day, the fire had been allowed to die down. Now he kicked the remaining logs aside to blacken harmlessly on the hearth.

He turned and caught Margaret watching

him. In spite of herself she looked scared. He spoke gravely.

"You must not be afraid of what is to come now. Do as I have bidden you, and you will surely be safe. If the enchantment is stronger than I know, then you have your knife, Hans. And you, little maid, shall have this." And he reached into the cupboard again and took from it a wooden box filled with what Margaret recognized as pepper.

"Even a forest wolf would quail before this," he said, with a wry look. "It is a powerful spice, and one of great value. Old Gulda had a taste for spices and strong relishes, so when Otho and I served our turn as pages at the Duke's table, we contrived—do not ask me how!—to bring her such things from time to time. She used them sparingly, and some of her hoard still remains here." He took a pinch, sniffed at it cautiously, then grimaced. "As I hoped, it has lost none of its power. So, costly though it is, do not scruple to use it! You promise me this?"

"I promise."

He handed her the box, then shut the cupboard door. "And now we must make ready. Go into the inner room, and bar the door as I have told you, and put up the shutters on the window. Try not to be afraid of me. That would be the bitterest thing of all, were I to harm you, or even make you fear me."

The children went into the inner room. Just as the door closed behind them Margaret saw Mardian turn away, not looking at them, his shoulders stiff and his head bent as if he was nerving himself for what was to come. On a sudden impulse she ran back to him, and took his hand between both of hers.

"Don't worry any more, dear Wolf. We're not afraid, and we'll manage. We know what to do, and we'll do exactly as you say. I—I hope it doesn't hurt too much."

His hand closed tightly over hers. "Tonight will be the first night that I have not suffered it quite alone. Good night, little maid. Good night, Hans. We shall see each other later in the night, but I shall not be able to speak with you. Now I wish you good fortune for the morrow."

They left him then, and shut the door. They ran to push the heavy chest up against it, and drive in the peg that held the latch fast. Then they barred the shutters, and, holding hands rather tightly, sat down on the chest to wait.

John heard it first. A sort of sliding thud, as if a heavy body had fallen to the floor, then the moaning, very soft, but somehow so terrible that he wanted to cover his ears to shut it out. Suddenly, as if it had been chopped off, the moaning stopped, to be followed by an even more dreadful silence. Then came a new sound, a long, whining yawn as if a big animal had just woken from sleep. There came the scratch and scrabble of claws on the wooden floor. Then a new kind of whining, eager and savage, and after that a long, soft snarl that raised the hairs along their

arms and made them clutch each other's hands
more tightly than before, and turn on their un-
comfortable perch to watch the door.

The paws approached it, with a stealthy click-
ing of claws on wood. Something sniffed and
snuffled along the gap at the bottom of the door.
More whining, and a slavering sort of howl, that
choked off sharply as the heavy body hurled
itself at the door.

The stout door creaked, rattled, and held
firm. Once, twice, the wolf flung his full weight
against it, his great claws raking down the
planks, his breath coming short and hard and
snarling. The children ran from the door, across
the dark room, to crouch under the shuttered
window. John had his knife drawn ready, and
Margaret clutched the pepper-box with shaking
fingers. They crouched there, their eyes on the
gap at the bottom of the door, where the wild
brute that was the enchanted Mardian leaped
and howled for their blood.

He went at last. They heard him race across
the room and out into the garden. But just as
they drew breaths of relief, he was there at the
window beside them. He could reach it easily.
His claws rattled the shutters. The whining
breaths were almost in their ears. They ran
again, this time to a far corner of the room, and
huddled there.

He had warned them, but they had expected
nothing like this. They began for the first time
to understand the full cruelty of Mardian's fate.
During the day he slept, or ate sparingly of

black bread with cheese or honey, but every
night this gentle and noble man was doomed to
hunt and kill some living thing. Worse than
that, he was doomed each day to remember what
he had done, and to think of it, not like a real
wolf, but like a man. He had locked the children
away like this because he had known the awful
frenzy that would overtake him, and the real
danger the children risked from him. If he were
even to scratch them with those dreadful claws,
he would suffer from it as much as they. But he
could not help himself...

Then suddenly it was all over. The wolf left
the window. They did not hear him cross the
garden, but from the dark forest beyond the
ruined wall they heard the long, eerie wolf-howl
that lifts the hairs along the hearer's spine.
Then silence.

A long silence, and the hooting of the owl.

The children went back to sit on the clothes-
chest, and to watch the cracks in the shutters
for the rising of the moon.

It rose perhaps an hour later. It seemed a
very long hour to John and Margaret, waiting
in the dark with nothing to do, and only the
coming adventure—which now seemed distinctly real and rather frightening—to talk
about. But at last the moonlight showed, white
and strong, between the shutters, and they
could unfasten them, and watch for Wolf's return.

At length he came.

One moment the clearing was quite empty, with moonlight falling on the tangled brambles, and the foxglove spires standing up like silver ghosts; the next, the wolf was there, trotting out from the cover of the pines into the white moonlight. They could see him as clearly as if it were day, the gleaming eyes, the lolling tongue, and the black smears of blood on his jaws and chest. Neither then nor at any other time did they let themselves wonder what he had found to kill and eat, but he had certainly fed. He slipped quietly across the ruined wall into the cottage garden, then turned aside to put his muzzle down to the long, wet grass, and rolled, cleaning the horrible stains from his coat. That done, he stood and shook himself, then trotted to the cottage door and looked sideways up towards their window, with one paw raised, like a dog asking to be let in.

"He wants us to come out now." Margaret's voice was not exactly shaking, but it was not steady.

"Well, so we come out," said John, rather gruffly. "And silly idiots we'd look, wouldn't we, if it wasn't the right wolf?"

But it was the right wolf. They hauled the chest away from the door, pulled the peg out and lifted the latch and went out, rather cautiously, into the other room. He was waiting for them there. He was bigger even than they remembered, bigger than any ordinary wolf, far bigger than their dog Tray. His shoulders were level with Margaret's chest, and if his head was up, his eyes could meet hers on a level. But his head was down as he faced them, and his tail, too. He was remembering what his wolf's nature had made him do, and with his man's brain he was ashamed.

I think it was at that moment that the children, without saying anything to one another, first realized how much they hated the false enchanter. However it was done, he had to be destroyed. However it had to be done, they would do it. Men who so imprison and degrade other men deserve the worst.

Neither of the children made any attempt to touch Wolf or caress him, as one would a dog. John slipped the knife back into its sheath, and Margaret went quietly to put the pepper-box back on its shelf in the cupboard. Then they picked up their cloaks—John's black and his sister's dark brown—and put them on.

John tapped his pouch. "I've got the amulet safe," he told the wolf.

"And I've got food in case we need it," said Margaret, showing the big pocket inside her cloak. She added carefully, just as she would have done if he had still been the Duke's counsellor: "We are ready now, Lord Mardian."

The werwolf turned and trotted out into the moonlight, and the children followed him.

CHAPTER NINE

The last time the children had gone up through the forest they had been running in fear from the wolf. Now they went with Wolf himself for their guide and guardian. At first they could see very little, and went cautiously, waiting till their eyes grew used to the darkness. Once Margaret stumbled over a tree root and would have fallen, but the wolf was close beside her, and she only went to her knees, saving herself with an arm flung over his back. After that she kept a hand on his ruff. He, being a creature of the night, could see in darkness as well as any cat or owl.

The track turned uphill. They scrambled past

the fallen pine, and soon after that came out
into the white moonlight. There was the picnic
place, and the tree stump where the signpost
had stood. The children neither hesitated nor
spoke, but John did give one swift, sidelong look
at the tree stump, as if expecting to see something there. His look was more puzzled than
curious, but next moment he had forgotten what
had puzzled him, and trotted on with the others.
Presently they came to the place where the way
to the castle left the upper road.

The wolf stopped, and the children with him.
They stood bewildered. If the castle had been
whole and lighted, and buzzing with activity,
they would not have been surprised. But it was
not. It was a ruin, just as it had been before.

And this was the castle that Wolf wanted
them to enter for him, to find its Duke, and
plead with him for his friend's life? The two
children stared in amazement at the empty
shell of stone on its distant hill. Then looked at
the wolf, in pity and in dread.

Then something happened that really did
bring the gooseflesh out along their skin. The
wolf sat down, lifted his grey head towards the
moon, and once more let out that long, terrible
howl. The sound spoke of grief and terror and
immense loneliness, and it filled the night. The
children, clutching one another's hands, found
themselves backing away from the savage sound.

Then, as suddenly as it had started, it stopped.
Wolf fell silent once more, and got to his feet.
His head was up and his ears alert. He threw

them a look over his shoulder, then trotted forward. He seemed undismayed by what they had seen. Margaret whispered: "It must be part of the enchantment. He forgot to tell us," and then they followed him down the track until it brought them almost to the edge of the moat.

Here Wolf stopped again. They waited.

Nothing moved. There was no sound or sign of life. Margaret looked across the reedy mud of the moat at the rocks out of which the castle walls seemed to grow like cliffs. The place was a deserted ruin. There were eyeless windows where saplings grew, and stars showed through the arches of some tower that must once have been the bell-tower of a chapel. The castle's turrets still thrust up against the sky, some of them broken, but others still showing the pointed witches' hats of their roofs gleaming to the moon. The castle's great gate gaped open, giving on a deserted and rubble-filled courtyard. In the top of the archway showed the rusting spikes of a portcullis. Approaching this, a narrow wooden causeway led across the mud of the moat. It looked rotten, and in places had crumbled to nothing. It stopped some twenty feet short of the gateway. There had once been a drawbridge across the gap; now there was nothing but a pair of snapped and rotting chains.

The wolf moved. He slipped silently off the track, which was here banked up for the approach to the causeway, and slunk, low to the ground, into the deep shadow under the bank. The children followed him, not understanding

the need for caution, but crouching down and
moving carefully. When all three were hidden
in the shadow below the bank, Wolf led them
forward, right to the edge of the moat. He did
not pause there, but, throwing another glance
over his shoulder at the children, inched forward into the reeds.

It was an unpleasant crossing. The wolf went
ahead, trying the surface and showing them the
way, but still they got their feet soaked and
their hose muddy, before at length they scrambled out on the far side. Here Wolf turned
sharply away to the left, into the shadow of a
crumbling buttress. They followed him, scrambling up to the very roots of the castle wall.
Clinging to the rough stones, they crept on
round the foot of the wall, until at length Wolf
stopped once more, and crouched, waiting.

When they came up with him they saw that
beside him, half hidden by a tangle of ivy and
elderberry, was a barred window. It was only
a foot or so above ground level. It was the kind
of half-window that one can sometimes see
throwing light into a basement. This must be
the window to Wolf's secret room. His yellow
eyes were fixed on them, gleaming in the moonlight. He panted with tiny whining sounds, as
if he could not help himself. They could guess,
from the way he looked at the window grating,
then back at the children, that once more he
was suffering from the helpless frustration that
tortured the once powerful Lord Mardian.

John fell on his knees by the window, and

laid hold of the rusty grating. Margaret ran to help him, but there was no need. In a couple of tugs the grating came loose, as if, without the rust to hold it in place, it might have fallen from the frame long since. It lifted out cleanly, like a square of trellis. John laid it aside. Wolf went past him like a shadow, and vanished into the black gap. With the barest hesitation, John followed, and then Margaret heard him whisper:

"Come on. It's all right. There's nobody here."

As if he needed to tell me that, thought Margaret, as she in her turn crept through the window frame. John reached to help her. She wriggled through, reached the floor, and stood up. Then she saw what John meant. The ruined castle they had seen, the crumbling causeway, the empty moat—all these were, indeed, part of the enchantment; an enchantment that stopped at the walls. Now that they were inside, the castle was complete, occupied, furnished, just as the real Mardian had known it. The secret room, though dusty and apparently unused, was dry and showed no signs of decay. As her eyes grew used to the dark she could see a table in the middle of the room, a chair and a stool, some empty shelves, and a big cupboard like a wardrobe. And in a corner of the opposite wall, a door, with a heavy iron latch.

Wolf gave one look round the room, as if remembering things long forgotten, then ran straight to the door. He flung that look of command at John. The boy lifted the latch, and carefully began to open the door, waiting all the

time for the betraying creak of unused hinges.
But there was none. The door opened quietly.

Cautiously the children peered out. All was
well. Wolf had told them that the secret room
opened into the castle cellars, and now they
found themselves looking out between the shapes
of two enormous vats of wine. A ladder stood
against the nearer of the vats, showing where
the cellarer had been up to lift the lid and test
the contents. Dust was thick on the floor boards,
and cobwebs hung festooned everywhere. The
walls of the cellar were lined with wooden
planks roughly pegged together, and the outside
of the secret door was covered with these, so
that, when it was shut, there was nothing to
betray its existence but the thin cut in the
planks across the top of the door. There was no
handle, only a knothole in the wood, where a
finger, inserted, could find the peg of the latch.
The door was placed between the two vats far-
thest from the window, so that even when the
cellarer came with his candle or horned lantern,
the vats threw shadows so big and black that
no secret door could be suspected.

Wolf had told them that the cellars and storerooms stretched right under this part of the castle. They could see, dimly, that the place was
very big. It was in plan like a huge stable, with
stalls twenty feet wide and as deep again, bay
after bay of barrels and bottles and jars, and
locked chests of grain and salted meat. The
place was a silent, echoing vault of darkness,
smelling deliciously of wine and grain and

spices. Somewhere a tub of yeast scented the air. Faint scurrying told of the presence of mice, and perhaps (thought Margaret, with a quickening pulse) rats. Once, when there was a scurry and a squeak near at hand, she felt the wolf beside her tense and crouch; then he relaxed, she could imagine how sheepishly, and became Wolf again, leading them forward past the bays of chests and bales and bottles.

They turned a corner, and there ahead of them was a wide stone stairway lit by another half-window, with its grating still in place. There was no glass. Cool night air came in, and with it the rays of the moon, lighting the steps. At the top was a big door, which was shut. They ran up the steps, and John took the great iron handle in both hands. He had to use a fair amount of strength to lift it. Like the door of the secret room, this one opened silently. Again, the children peered through.

They saw what Wolf had told them to expect: a wide stone corridor, lit by a torch which hung, smoking and spluttering a bit, in an iron bracket. There were doorways to left and right, but the doors were all shut. Beyond the torch they could see, faintly, that the corridor was barred by another door. This would open into the lobby between the kitchens and the great hall. It was the way they would have to go tomorrow.

But tonight they must stay hidden. They turned to go back to the secret room. This time the wolf did not go ahead to guide them. He lingered for a moment, looking back at the shut door of what had once been his familiar home. Then, slowly, he began to follow the children down the steps. He reached the window. He stopped abruptly in the patch of bright moonlight and sat back on his haunches. His head went up.

"Quick! He's going to howl!" gasped John.

In a flash Margaret was on her knees beside Wolf, and her arms were round his neck. "Wolf! Wolf, dear! Hush! You must not!"

She could feel the dreadful sound welling up in the wolf's throat, as if from some deep spring of grief in his body. Then he checked, swallowed, and his teeth clicked shut on the sound before it was born. The grey head moved, the tongue licked Margaret's cheek like a kiss, and he ran down ahead of them, out of the moonlight, and back through the dark cellar.

The three of them slipped through the narrow gap between the sixth and seventh vats. The door of the secret room shut behind them. Wolf ran to the window, and paused with his paws on the sill, ready to leave them.

"We'll remember everything," promised John. "We'll be all right, really, sir."

"We'll be terribly careful," Margaret assured him, "and the spell's sure to work beautifully, so please don't worry."

"And don't try to come back in daylight, whatever happens," added John. "I'll put the grating back now, and we'll come down here every night if we can, and let you in."

"And perhaps quite soon," finished Margaret softly, "the Duke himself will be here with us, waiting for you. Dear Wolf, take care. We really will do just as you told us."

The wolf slanted one long, last look at them, then turned and leaped through the window, and was gone. John climbed to the sill, leaned out and lifted the grating, and wedged it back into place. Seconds later, from somewhere not far off, they heard the long, sobbing howl of the wolf in moonlight.

"Goodness! Look!" exclaimed John.

Margaret knelt on the sill beside him, and they looked out together.

The moon, high and full, lighted the steep rocky slope down to the moatside. But where they had picked their way across through the mud and rushes, there stretched, now, a wide expanse of shining water, girdling the castle. The causeway, unbroken, led across it, to disappear from their sight behind the castle buttress.

They were safe within the castle—within the spell. For them, at last, the world of Mardian and Duke Otho was complete. Though it was out of their sight they knew that the drawbridge, whole and new, would be drawn up against the gleaming portcullis. There would be flags flying from the towers, and gilded weathercocks catching the moonlight. There would be lights in the windows, and bustle in the courtyard. But for Wolf-Mardian, back on the far side of the moat, alone in his cruel enchantment, the palace of his lord had once more vanished, to be replaced by a wasted ruin.

They turned back and began to unpack the things they had brought. They dared not light a candle, but the glimpses of moonlight showed them enough. They found some bread and raisins, and ate them, each took a swig of the strong, sweet drink from the flask Mardian had given them, then they wrapped themselves in their warm cloaks, and resigned themselves to waiting till morning.

CHAPTER TEN

They had not thought they could sleep, but the excitement and strain of the day, and perhaps the enchantment, too, told on them. They fell soundly asleep, curled there on the floor, and slept until the morning sun sent a bright slanting beam through the window, and woke them.

John sat up, stretching, and yawned, then jumped up and ran to the window. Outside, bright in the sunlight, glittered the wide water of the moat, and across the causeway, clattering and calling, came carts and people.

"Like a market," said Margaret, at his elbow. "They're bringing things in to sell to the castle people, eggs and vegetables and things. There's

a donkey with panniers, and big jars in them.
I wonder what's in the jars? And look, there's
a peddler, with a tray slung round his neck."

"And a cart with oxen," said her brother.
"And—oh, here's the hunt coming back! They
must have been out again at dawn. We never
heard them. I wonder—I suppose they were
after Wolf again."

Both children craned to look. The market people were making way for the gay troop of riders
who clattered now over the causeway. There
were the hounds, there the chief huntsman on
his big bay horse, and there was the same lady
dressed in green. "And the prince," said Margaret. "That must be the prince. See, on the
white horse. He's awfully like his father—the
young man on Wolf's amulet. Well, they haven't
caught Wolf. They've got nothing with them.
We'd see easily from here, if they had."

And if they have killed him down there in the
forest, thought John, we shan't know until tonight, when he doesn't come back here to the
window. And by then it may be too late for us.
But he said none of this aloud. He turned from
the window, and began to tidy his clothes. "We'd
better get out of here. Everyone's around now,
and if there's a crowd it'll be easier to mix in
and not be noticed. Did you say you'd brought
a comb? After you. Thanks. Now, we'd better go
if we want something to eat. Remember, Wolf
said everyone got up terribly early, and they
have dinner at about nine, and then nothing

more till suppertime. I wonder what they have? I'm hungry enough to eat anything."

"Probably just as well. It'll be things like herring pie and lampreys and boars' heads and small beer," said Margaret.

"Whatever it is, I hope there's lots of it. And large beer, too, for choice. Let's go, then. We've got it all straight, haven't we? If we get separated, or if things get tricky, we meet again here. And back here at night, anyway, if it's possible. Right?"

"Right. Let's get it over, and the sooner the better, I'm starving....Only," added Margaret, "let's find what Wolf called the privy chamber first, shall we? I've forgotten which door it was on the plan."

"The third, in the passage upstairs. It'll only be a hole in the floor, if it's anything like ones I've seen in mediaeval ruins before. Margaret—"

"What?"

"It's queer, isn't it, the way we can be still ourselves—you know what I mean, looking at all this as if it was still something in a storybook—and yet at the same time we sort of look right and we know how to talk, and more or less what to expect....And have *you* more or less forgotten what happened before we met Wolf? I have, just about. I do remember something about a note left on a tree stump..."

Margaret nodded solemnly. "It's the same with me. I don't remember any note, but there was a blanket on the grass somewhere, and we

found a sweetmeat—chocolate, that's it—
and...and that's about all I do remember. It
must be an awfully powerful spell. Which is just
as well," she finished, "because it's got to stop
anyone in the castle guessing about us, and it's
my guess this is going to be a pretty difficult
day."

"You're telling me," said her brother. "Well,
come on, let's get started. If we don't go now
there'll be nothing till supper, remember!"

They peeped out of the secret door. There was
no one about, no sound, no movement. They
made their way through the cellar, up the steps,
and out into the deserted corridor beyond. They
found the privy chamber—which was, indeed,
just a tiny stone room with a hole in the floor
leading down, presumably, into the moat—and
then tiptoed along the corridor, and let themselves cautiously through the second door.

And here their luck ran out. They turned a
corner to find themselves face to face with a
man in a long blue robe, who wore a flat cap
with a silver buckle, and carried a parchment
roll and a bunch of keys. Behind him were two
other men, young, in plain russet clothes that
looked like servants' livery. The eagle badge
was worked in yellow on the breasts of their
tunics.

The children stopped dead. So did the man,
looking at them in surprise. At least, thought
John, bracing himself for what was to come, it
isn't the enchanter. Wolf told us he looked exactly like him, like Mardian. And it can't pos-

sibly be the Duke. More like a steward or something, and on his way to the cellars for the small beer...He wanted to laugh, and this stopped him from being frightened. He took Margaret's hand and looked up at the man, half laughing, half scared—exactly the look of a boy caught out in some not very bad mischief.

This was how the steward, for such he was, read it.

"What are you doing here, boy?" he asked sharply. "Why are you not in the hall with the rest? God's wounds, is there not enough work for you all, with the serving? And my lords just back from hunting, and hungry enough to eat their horses?"

"I'm sorry, sir. I was just on my way. And did—and did the hunt find their quarry?"

"The great wolf?" The man laughed. "Not they. No sight of him this dawning, so they say. So he still roams the woods, my young cockerel, to eat disobedient children. Where have you been? And what is this wench doing here?"

"Please, sir, she is my sister."

At that moment a large lady in black, with a headdress horned like a Highland cow, swept into the corridor, saw Margaret, and gave a little scream, half of anger, half of shock.

"The shameless wench! The little hussy! Well, my young madam, and what do you here?"

"It was the little dog, madam." Margaret had had time to think, but even so, she spoke so glibly that she surprised even herself.

"What little dog?"

"Please, madam, I do not know. But I saw it running this way, and thought it was one of my lord's, and was lost, so I ran after it, and—"

"And I saw my sister coming here, so ran after her to fetch her back," said John virtuously.

The steward eyed him doubtfully, then gave a nod.

"Well, there's naught here for you to steal. And if I find a single box moved, or cask broached in the cellarage yonder, I'll see you whipped myself. What's your name?"

"Hans, sir. The Lady Grisel is my grand-dame."

Another little shriek from the lady in black, who seized Margaret's arm and slapped her hand smartly. "Then all the more shame to you for running off like that! What would my Lady Grisel say—if she could say anything at all, that is, poor lady, with her wits so sadly astray! For which we may be thankful, perchance, for she need never know of such conduct. So come your ways, young madam, to the nurseries!" And before the children could exchange more than a look, she rustled off up the corridor, with Margaret firmly held in tow.

"And you, too, boy! Get you to the hall, and stir yourself about the serving. Begone, rascal!" snapped the steward, aiming a cuff for John's head. John dodged, and ran.

It was easy enough to tell where the hall and kitchens were, because of the noise. John paused in the doorway, staring, startled and a bit confused.

The great hall was an enormous room, with high arched windows blazing in the morning sun. Shafts of sunlight fell slanting along a floor thickly strewn with rushes, where dogs wrangled for food among people's feet. Down both sides of the hall were long narrow tables, at which people sat on benches, eating with their fingers from wooden platters. Across the far end of the hall was a raised dais with another table on it, which ran the width of the room. This table was covered with a white cloth, and here sat men and women better dressed, who ate off silver. At the center of this table was a tall chair with a high carved back, like a throne, and in it sat a man who must be the Duke. The dishes in front of him were of gold, and there was a big gold vessel beside him, shaped beautifully like a ship. Without knowing how, John recognized this for the nef, the precious vessel filled with spices to season the Duke's meat. Near it stood the great saltcellar, marvellously made from gold and silver for the Duke's own use. Above the great chair was a canopy draped with crimson silk and held by a great, carved golden eagle, with a crown on its head.

The Duke himself was soberly dressed in dark blue. On his head was a dark-blue velvet cap with a scarf of dusky crimson twisted round it, one end of which hung down over his shoulder. The cap was fastened with a gold brooch where a red stone flashed and sparkled. Another brooch glinted at his shoulder, and there were rings on his hands. He was turning a tall golden

goblet round and round in his fingers, and looking, thought John, sadder than anyone, even a
duke, ought to look. As sad, almost, as Wolf had
looked when they had first seen him.

He felt his breath shorten. For there, on the
Duke's left, in another tall chair almost as
grand as the Duke's own, sat Mardian.

In spite of all that Wolf had told him, it took
a few seconds for John to realize that this man,
"Mardian" in every detail, must be Almeric the
enchanter. It was all there, the dark thin face,
the narrow tawny eyes, the long, elegant hands,
the slant of the head and the grave courtesy
with which he said something to the Duke beside him. The Duke turned slightly, inclining
himself to listen. Something swung, glinting,
on his breast. John drew in his breath. Round
the Duke's neck he could see the heavy wrought-
gold chain, and on his breast the amulet.

Without even thinking about it, John found
that his hand had slid into the pouch at his belt,
and he was fingering Mardian's amulet. So
Duke Otho wanted to forget his displeasure,
hoping, perhaps, that all might still be well between himself and his old friend. He still wore
the token. There was hope, then, for the "faith
and trust" on which Mardian had ventured the
children's safety and his own life.

The enchanter spoke again, smiling. The
Duke nodded, with an answering smile, but
somehow his face was still sad. He gave a half-
glance at the chair on his right, which stood
empty. The prince? He had been with the hunt-

ing party. No doubt the enchanter was waiting, with some eagerness, to know if Wolf had been caught and killed. The Duke, indifferent, had gone back into his silent musing. John's fingers tightened on the amulet. Just you wait, Almeric, just you wait. If the Duke only knew...

He was shaken rudely out of his thoughts. A steward, bustling past with a platter of steaming food, called sharply: "You, boy! Look sharp and serve at the kitchen end!"

John saw then that a positive stream of boys, dressed much as he was, were hurrying to and fro between the tables and the big door at the foot of the hall. He ran after them, and found himself in the kitchens. He had no time for more than a quick sight of the high, blackened roof, the gaping caves of the chimneys where great fires blazed, and cooks, sweating and scarlet-faced, basted and stirred, or heaved great trays of hot pasties and pies out of the ovens. Someone thrust a dish into his hands, and he grabbed it and turned to follow the nearest boy back into the hall.

The next hour or so was a blur. People seemed to eat as much as lions in a zoo, and drink goblet after goblet of ale or wine to wash the food down. There was not time to be nervous, or to worry about being discovered. No one even noticed him except to hand food to him or to tell him to hurry, or to bring more. He began to enjoy himself. He grew neat-handed, and, after almost falling flat on his face in the dirty rushes when one of the dogs fled yapping under his

feet, he learned to thread his way among the
dogs, and to dodge the other hurrying servants
and pages. He learned, too, to dodge the bones
and other scraps which the diners flung over
their shoulders when they had finished gnaw-
ing them. He even, like the other boys, managed
to grab a few good pieces for himself off the
platters, and gobble them quickly and greedily
in the few moments of waiting in the kitchens.
The food was good, hot and spicy, and strange
to his palate, but after the excitements of the
night and morning he felt ravenous. He wondered if Margaret had managed to get dinner,
too, but he did not have time to worry about
her. What worried him was the growing knowl-
edge that his chances of coming anywhere near
the Duke were very slender indeed. The high
table was served—on bended knee—by stew-
ards and pages in black velvet trimmed with
silver. By the Duke's chair stood a page with a
crown embroidered on the breast of his tunic;
he was a slightly built, fair boy of John's own
age. He handed the Duke's food and poured his
wine, then knelt with a steaming silver bowl
while his master washed his hands and dried
them on a white napkin. No one else came near
the Duke at all. At the back of the dais was
ranged the body-guard, a dozen fully armed
men, whose spears glinted in the sunlight. It
was plain that Duke Otho's servants were spe-
cially chosen, and equally plain that the ducal
chamberlains watched them carefully all the
time. The Duke himself paid no attention to

them. He ate little, and spoke less, and John never saw him address anyone but the false enchanter at his left hand.

And Almeric? He sat back in his chair, attentive to anything the Duke said, but apparently watching—and noticing—all that went on in the hall. Occasionally his glance rested on the prince's empty chair, and then his smile deepened. John found it hard not to watch him, but he was sure that Almeric had not noticed him among the crowd of other bustling pages. Why should he? He could hardly know all the boys in the castle. So John ran, and served, and snatched food as he went, and wondered how on earth he was ever to come near the Duke, and what on earth had happened to Margaret.

CHAPTER ELEVEN

When Margaret and John made jokes about "only a girl," they were meant as jokes. But now, as she was scolded, and slapped, and hustled off to the women's rooms, she saw how, in the past, girls really had had something to complain about. The lady in black seemed to think it downright wicked of her to have been found near the kitchen quarters, talking to her own brother. She read Margaret a long lecture on modesty, which apparently meant sitting still on a hard chair with your back straight, your hands in your lap, and your eyes cast down, "when any man speaks to you, young madam, remember that!"

Even John? thought Margaret furiously, but trying to find it funny. She bit her lip on what she would have liked to say, and concentrated on keeping her head and her temper, and on memorizing the maze of corridors and stairways that led in the end to the women's side of the castle. There, among the girls and nurses and tumbling babies of the "nurseries," she was pushed with a sharp command to "Stay here, madam, and mind your manners, or it will be a whipping the next time you're found straying where you have no business!"

Like John, she found that there were so many people that she was hardly noticed. The castle was, in fact, like a small town or a large, over-crowded village: it had a big mixed population who did not all know each other. When one of the nursemaids asked her who she was, she told the story of "my Lady Grisel" as Wolf had bidden her, and the woman only nodded, looking a bit sorry for her, and told her to get to table and break her fast, then go out into the garden to join the others at ball.

"Ball" was what she would have called pig-in-the-middle, and she was rather good at it. The garden was a wide strip of grass, with flower beds along the edges, and, on the side away from the castle, a low battlemented wall edging a steep drop to another garden below. The lower garden was also edged by battlements, and a long, straight drop to the moat. There seemed to be no way down; it must be out of bounds, at any rate to the girls.

The game went on, the other girls ran, and threw and called. The sun was warm, and the beds were full of scented flowers, roses, jasmine, pinks. Some ladies walked in the sun, others sat on the seats along the terrace walks and talked or sewed, while the children, with kilted skirts, played on the grass. The ladies' dresses were beautiful, in rich blues and greens and shades of rose, with long flowing sleeves lined with embroidery. Their hair was braided up under pretty coronets, or elaborate headdresses from which white veils fluttered in the breeze. It was all very charming, very colourful, and very boring. Margaret thought enviously of John, on the livelier side of the castle, and wondered how he was getting on. Somehow or other it looked less and less possible for John and herself to help poor Wolf. Getting here had been exciting, and rather easy, and becoming part of the castle's bustling life had been easy, too. But it was hard to see what she could do here. It didn't look, she thought crossly, as if she would even get a sight of the Duke. If she had to spend all her time with the women and girls, then all Wolf's plans for her had been for nothing. She could not even help John...

She missed an easy catch, and there were shrieks from the other children. The ball, flying past her, shot over the low battlement that edged the garden. Angry with herself for attracting attention, Margaret ran to see where it had gone. It had landed on the lawn below.

She leaned over. There was a boy, a youth of

about fourteen, sitting in the sun on a stone seat at the foot of the wall. He stuck out a foot, and fielded the ball as it rolled to his feet.

"Here!" called Margaret.

She thought there was surprise on the boy's face as he looked up, but he smiled pleasantly and threw the ball. She caught it, then threw it as hard as she could to the far side of the upper garden. The other children ran after it. For the moment, no one was looking at her. Quietly, picking up her skirts, she slipped behind a thick bush of myrtle, where there was a stone seat by the terrace wall. She sat there, twisting her body to crane over and watch the garden below. All at once, things had become more interesting. The boy who had returned the ball was someone she had seen before. Prince Crispin himself.

"Modesty," said Margaret to herself. "I'll show them modesty! I'm far too modest to play silly ball games on the lawn. If anyone sees me here I shall fold my hands and sit as straight as a poker and look at the ground.... But in the meantime I'm going to have a real good look at the prince."

Yes, it was the same boy. He looked, she thought, rather nice, but a bit pale and perhaps sickly. Now that he was no longer smiling his face was heavy and his eyes dull. He had sat down again, and was busy pulling a sprig of jasmine to shreds in his fingers. He seemed to be waiting for someone.

There was a sound of footsteps. The boy

looked up and his face altered. A man, walking fast, was coming along the path towards him. It was Almeric, the enchanter. Though Margaret knew straight away who this must be, she, like her brother, could hardly believe that the tall man with the dark hair and tawny eyes was only a shadowy copy of Wolf-Mardian. He looked up, and for a moment she felt a shock of real fear, as if he could look right through the tangled boughs of myrtle and see her watching him. But he looked away immediately and spoke to the youth.

That was another shock. It was one thing seeing the man who looked exactly like Mardian; it was another hearing Mardian's own voice, grave and steady and kind, just within a few feet of her. Margaret's heart gave a bound, then quickened to a fast beat of excitement. She might, after all, be going to learn something of value. She sat as still as a mouse in the shadow of the myrtle bush, listening.

She had missed the first word or two. The prince was speaking: "—Not hungry," he was saying, sounding rather surly, or perhaps just unhappy.

"What talk is this?" came Mardian's voice. "Are we to have people thinking that you, too, are ailing?"

"What does it matter what they think? It sickens me, going into the hall. My father does not seem to notice, but I see them all...watching him all the time, sideways, as if they are wondering if he will even live long enough for me to reach my name-day." The prince's voice changed. "Where do these rumours come from, Mardian, tell me that? He is lame, yes. He is sometimes in pain, yes. But he is not sick, and he is very far from dying. So why do men like Brand and Osric and the rest come fawning near me all day, and what are they saying to you, when they crowd in corners and whisper behind their hands?"

"No more than that they are troubled about the Duke your father." The grave voice hesitated, as if reluctant to go on. Then Almeric continued: "As you have just said, your name-day is near, and on that day you must be reckoned fit to govern beside your father...or, if need be, alone. So you must be man enough now to bear the truth."

"What truth?"

"That Duke Otho is indeed sick, and, if no cure can be found soon, is even likely to die. You may be Duke yourself sooner than you had imagined."

There was a short, shocked pause, then the boy's voice: "I don't believe it! Mardian, you must be wrong! The physicians—"

"The physicians have done all they can, and now they shake their heads."

"I know! Do you think I have not spoken with them myself? They hum and haw and pull their beards, but it's my belief that they have no idea what ails him! And what could it be, that these learned men cannot recognize and treat? Melancholy, they call it....Well, but melancholy is not a sickness! And where does it come from? It cannot be grief for my mother. All grief passes, and it is two years now. Why can he not put grief aside? Besides, we have spoken together about it, and he said it was not that. He cannot explain it himself. He is like a man drugged, or drowning, he says, who cannot summon up the strength to strike out for shore. May I ask you a question?"

"Of course."

"You do not—the Duke and you are reconciled, are you not?"

"Reconciled? When did we ever quarrel, to need a reconciliation?"

"He has spoken bitterly to you, you know that."

"It is his right," said the false Mardian. "Do you not know me well enough to know that my love and loyalty have never wavered?"

(Pig, thought Margaret. Pig.)

It seemed that something in the enchanter's voice did not ring quite true, even to Crispin. He must have shown it, for Almeric added, rather sharply: "Why do you ask? What has the Duke said? Have I not been the same to him as ever?"

There was a brief pause. "Of course," said Crispin.

"This talk of drugs—" The enchanter spoke forcefully. "How could the Duke be drugged? He eats with his other lords, and all his food and wine is served to him by either Denis or Justin, the two ducal pages. They are totally to be trusted—and besides, they taste everything themselves. Drugs? Nonsense!"

"Of course," said the prince again, quite without expression. "That's exactly what the Duke's chief physician said, when I talked with him this morning."

"You talked with him? But, my dear boy, I told you to leave such matters with me...with his advisers. What did he tell you?"

"He could tell me nothing, except that it seemed as if the Duke was under enchantment."

Almeric laughed. "But this is nonsense, too. He was jesting!"

"Perhaps. He said that he could see no reason for the sickness. It was like a spell that takes away the will to do, or even to live. My father's limbs are not withered, yet he cannot walk. Had he the will, the doctors say, he could stand, and in due time learn to walk again. And certainly he could ride. Yet for years now he has kept within the castle, and will try nothing and go nowhere. Does this not seem like enchantment to you, Mardian?"

There was another pause. Then Almeric spoke, slowly. "You are right. I was wrong to try and keep the truth from you. This 'melancholy' of your father's...you say it is not a sickness, but you are wrong. It is like a fell disease, which takes away the very will to live. There is a name for it. Men call it the 'wolf-sickness.' Have you not heard the name? Why do you think we ride out daily to catch and slay the cruel beasts that harry the peasants' stock, and spread the disease abroad, the wolf's plague?"

"For sport, I thought." The prince sounded surprised.

"Yes, but for more than that. I tell you, Crispin, that if we could but catch and slay that great wolf, then the lesser beasts of the pack would leave the forest, and the sickness would abate."

"You mean, my father would get better?"

"Who can say? But for almost two years now the great wolf has ravaged the countryside, and the Duke has been a sick man."

"If that isn't magic, what is?"

"Magic lies in belief," said Almeric.

"And my father would believe this himself?"

"Why should he not? The doctors will tell him there is something in it. All learned men know of the wolf-sickness. And all men know that evil men can change themselves into wolves, and bring death and destruction."

"Like Almeric," said the prince.

(Up in her hiding place, Margaret jumped as if pricked with a pin.)

Almeric must have done the same. His voice sharpened. *"Like whom?"*

"Don't you remember him? That vile character who left the court rather suddenly a couple of years ago. My father distrusted him—and so did you. I remember hearing you say so."

"Ah, yes, I remember now."

"You remember he vanished quite suddenly?

Perhaps he turned himself into a wolf. Perhaps—"

"This is fool's talk," snapped Almeric.

"I think you forget yourself!" Crispin's voice changed. (I do believe he dislikes him, for all he thinks this is Mardian, thought Margaret.)

There was a sharp pause. Then the enchanter said humbly: "Forgive me, my prince. I spoke too hastily. But all this talk of magic—"

"Well, but you spoke of it yourself, of men changing themselves into wolves. I was only repeating what some of the people are saying. Osric told me that once he'd heard Almeric speak about magic arts, and he was wondering if Almeric himself could be the great wolf."

(And put *that* in your pipe and smoke it! thought Margaret, hugging herself behind the myrtle boughs.)

There was silence below. Perhaps Almeric could think of nothing to say. It was the prince who went on, briskly: "You're right, that's foolishness. But talking of the great wolf...seriously, Mardian, I've had an idea. My father was asking only yesterday how I would like to celebrate my name-day, apart from the usual ceremonies. Why don't I say that what I'd really like is a grand ducal hunt? A wolf-hunt, lasting all day until the time for feasting? If I could persuade him, for my sake, to venture out in a litter, even a short way, just to watch the hunt—"

"No!"

"Why not?" Crispin sounded surprised. "I'd have thought we should try anything that

would persuade him to venture outside the
walls once more, and the next time it will be
easier. If he himself believes this sickness could
be magical, then the sight of the great wolf itself—and perhaps that day we might be lucky
and catch him..."

His voice trailed off, enquiringly. Margaret
would have given a lot to be able to see the
enchanter's face. When at length he spoke, his
voice was as smooth and pleasant as ever. "Of
course you are right. It was my anxiety and love
for your father that made me protest. Let us
talk about it later, my dear prince, and not a
word to anyone else; this is our secret. Indeed,
anything that might bring Otho out of his settled melancholy is to be tried. But for you, with
your great day so near at hand...do not count
too much on anything. What you are best to do
is to fit yourself to help your father rule, and
then, one day, to succeed him. Like you, I must
put my grief aside, and think of the future,
when I can care for you and stand your friend,
as I have done in the past. Will you not accept
this friendship, and forget the doubts which
sometimes, lately, I have felt, to my sorrow?"

"A man who does not accept friendship is a
fool," said the prince. His voice was still rather
crisp. "But a prince who trusts any man without
proof is a fool. Will you give me proof of your
love, Mardian?"

"What more can I give? Another amulet?"
asked that gentle, rueful voice.

(The swine, thought Margaret, behind the

myrtle boughs. She craned farther. She could just see them. The prince had got to his feet. The two of them were moving away, their voices growing fainter.)

"That was one trust I mislaid," said the enchanter.

"No, not an amulet, your oath."

"Which you'll have in any case in a few days' time when your name-day comes? But of course. I will swear anything to you, any time, my prince. But let the swearing be private. Should the Duke come to hear of it, he might well think that you and I were too quick..."

The voices faded. But in any case Margaret would have heard no more. Footsteps sounded on the flagstones just beside the myrtle bush, and the swish of a skirt. The Highland Cow! She switched round on the seat, straightened her back and sat, hand in lap, eyes down, the very picture of a modest young girl resting in the shade.

The footsteps stopped right in front of her. It was not the Highland Cow. The skirt was of grass-green silk. The trailing sleeves were lined with white fur. Margaret looked up, into the eyes of the lady who had ridden with the hunt.

CHAPTER TWELVE

The lady was dark and beautiful, with black hair bound with gold, and green eyes. The green eyes were staring very hard at Margaret. She spoke sharply. "What are you doing here? Why are you not with the others?"

Margaret realized, all at once, that the garden was quiet; the children had all gone. One or two of the ladies still sat there with their stitchery, and a couple of gardeners were working in a corner, being directed by an elderly woman in grey. But otherwise the place was empty.

"Madam, we were playing at ball, and I was too hot. I was resting. I will go now," said Margaret quickly, jumping to her feet.

The lady in green put out a hand to stop her. "A moment." The hand took Margaret by the chin, lifting her face. "Who are you, girl?"

"The Lady Grisel is my grand-dame," said Margaret. It was all she could do not to pull herself away. The lady's nails were sharp, scoring her chin.

The green eyes narrowed, consideringly. "I have seen you before, have I not?" asked the lady.

"Why, yes, madam," stammered Margaret. "Many a time, with the other children... You would not remember me, though we speak of you often—"

"Speak of me? Why?" demanded the lady.

Margaret widened her eyes in a look of innocence. "Why, because you are so beautiful. And your gowns . . . your mantles . . . you are the most beautiful of all the ladies in the castle, I think."

The cruel hand released her. The lady was smiling. "Well, little maid, I thank you!" But she still lingered, staring. "I could have sworn . . . the strangest thing . . . Have you ever been outside the castle, child?"

"Never, madam."

"And the Lady Grisel is your grand-dame. What is your name?"

"Gretta, madam."

"And your mother?"

Margaret drooped her head, whispering: "My mother, alas, is dead." She was wondering, wildly, if her own mother's name would do. Isobel—was Isobel a likely name? If the green lady checked with Lady Grisel, who, mercifully, was cuckoo, it was to be hoped she couldn't remember what her daughters and daughters-in-law had been called.

Then she was saved. A young woman in scarlet appeared at the other side of the garden. "Blancheflower!" she called, and the lady in green turned quickly, waving. "Coming!" She glanced back at Margaret. "Go your ways, sweet child."

She tripped off, and vanished in the shadow of a stone archway.

The sweet child stood quite still, with her long skirts clutched tightly in her hands. Her mind was racing. It would only be a matter of time before the green lady remembered where she had seen little Gretta, who "had never been outside the castle." Remembered her, standing at the fork in the track, with a boy, watching the hunt. Remembered her strange clothes, her most immodest ways, the silver coin she had accepted from the huntsman. And remembered that she had misdirected the wolf-hunters.

Even if no one guessed at the truth, things could get very awkward indeed for Gretta, who had lied, and been forward, and had misbehaved herself in every way. At the worst, discovery would mean betrayal for both children. At the least, it could mean punishment for herself. She had not liked the sound of that whipping she had been promised.

There was only one thing to do. Little as she

liked the idea, she must get back into hiding,
into the secret room, and wait till she saw John
again. Then they could decide what best to do.

She was lucky. Lady Blancheflower was nowhere to be seen. She managed to slip through
the crowded rooms unobserved. Someone—the
kindly nursemaid—called after her: "This way,
Gretta! Where are you going?"

"Taking a message for Lady Blancheflower!"
called Margaret, and waved, smiling, as she
ran.

Luckily, she remembered the way, and in a
few minutes found herself, breathless and alone,
running down the dim corridor that led to the
cellars. Somewhere away to one side she could
hear the noise from the kitchens. She let herself
into the cellar, and stole past the great sleeping
vats of wine. One, two . . . six, seven, here it was.
Like a rabbit bolting into a safe hole she slipped
in through the secret door and found herself
once more in Wolf's room.

Time went by. The sun left the window. The
light mellowed to late afternoon. Margaret grew
bored, and then hungry. She had been rather
too excited to eat much at "dinner"—which to
her had been breakfast-time—and now she
faced, with dismay, the prospect of waiting until
John came back to the secret room, after serving
supper in the great hall. Even then she could
not be sure that he would bring food with him.

She explored the room, of course, but the big
cupboard was locked. Not that there would be

food there, and the steward had said that everything in the storerooms was locked, too. She wondered if she dared venture out again and try, or even if she should go up for supper in the nurseries, and risk meeting Lady Blancheflower. But just as she made up her mind that, whatever happened, she must find food, she heard a stealthy sound outside the door, and the latch lifted.

It was John. And, wonder of wonders, he had brought food, lots of it. He unwrapped the linen napkins and put it out on the table. There was white bread, and some big pieces of poultry, a chunk of pasty, and some fruit and other things she did not recognize. But they were all food, and they smelled gorgeous.

"I didn't know if you'd get anything much in the nursery rooms," he said, "and there was masses in the kitchens. I'm afraid it's all cold now, but I thought we might as well stock up, because you never know—hey, you must be starving!"

"I am." Margaret bit into a pasty. "I suppose there was plenty, but I was too nervous to eat much. Then I suddenly realized I would probably have to miss supper, too. I've been sitting here planning how to break into the stores outside."

"Why d'you have to miss supper? What's happened?"

"No, you first. I say, this turkey's super! What a size! Go on. Why did you come down so early? Did someone suspect you?"

"It's not turkey. It's swan. And that bit's peacock. Meg, you should just *see* the way they do them up, all the feathers and tail, the lot! They're fixing them up now in the kitchens, ready for supper. Just wait till I have time to tell you everything! But we'd better exchange news first. No, no one suspects me. I really came down to get out of joining the boys' games in the courtyard!" He made a face. "You should see them! Black eyes and broken noses are the least of it! It's all war games, of course, mock fights and tilting at the quintain—that's a sort of tournament practice—and they really do hammer at it. The master-at-arms is in charge, and he's a really tough type. I don't think I'd have lasted very long there!"

"You might have. If the spell's really working, you might have been good at it. You're good at—" she paused, trying to remember, and failing, "—at games and things at home, aren't you?"

"Well, I didn't dare risk giving myself away. It was lucky I did come now, as it happens. I'll have to go back soon, anyway. Supper starts in about an hour, and I'm on a sort of team now. It's funny, the boys waiting at table are all nobles, not kitchen boys or servants or anything. They wait on their own fathers, even. Anyway I'm on a team. Nobody's bothered to ask me any questions. And three people have called me Lionel, so perhaps the real Lionel has left, or died, or something. Died, quite likely, because they talk as if lots of people die when they're only young. Perhaps I look a bit like this Lionel, or something? Anyway, it's all right, and I'm getting the hang of it, and nobody seems a bit suspicious. . . ."

He talked on while she ate, feeling better every minute. He finished: "In a way, if it wasn't so serious, it's a lot of fun—only I can't quite see how I'll ever get near the Duke."

"You couldn't just wait about, and seize the chance to run up and kneel down in front of him and ask for an audience? It sounds awfully simple, but sometimes the simplest things work best."

"I might, I suppose. But it's risky. If I chose the time badly, and Almeric was there, I could end up in the dungeon, or worse, and I don't feel like trying it."

"Then perhaps Denis or Justin will die young, and you'll be promoted to wait on the Duke," said Margaret, biting into a chunk of something sweet that smelled of almonds. "This is smashing, it's like marzipan."

"They call it marchpane. Must be the same thing. What do you mean, Denis and Justin? Are they the Duke's pages? I saw one of them waiting on him this morning, but I daren't ask his name, because people would have thought it funny that I didn't know. How do you know? What did you find out?"

"Not much, only that I think Wolf's wrong about the prince. I don't think he's Almeric's loving little lapdog at all. I think he suspects him of something, but doesn't know what. I overheard them talking."

"You did? Good for you! Tell me!"

"Actually, it was rather funny, if it hadn't made me so furious." And Margaret, with pauses for chewing, told John her story. She finished with the green lady, and her reasons for running away to hide.

Her brother said thoughtfully: "Pity. It might mean you do have to stay hidden here. Let's hope she doesn't spot me as well. That really might jog her memory. I'll have to keep out of the way when the hunt goes out tomorrow. But you—"

"If I have to stay locked in here, I might as well not be in the castle at all," said Margaret crossly. It really had been a very boring afternoon.

"All we can do is wait, and tell Wolf when he comes. He won't be able to talk to us, but he might want you to go back to the cottage with him."

"And leave you here alone?"

"I know. But it can't be for long."

"It might be days. Bother that green woman!"

A creaking noise, followed by a crash, drew them towards the window, to gaze out across the swan-furrowed moat. The drawbridge was being lifted. The castle was settling in for the night.

John spoke quickly. "Look, Meg, sorry, but I'll have to go. I'll bring more food down after supper. I'd better take the napkins back now. I'll be back in time for Wolf."

"You can't be sure of that. Supper might go on for ages. What about helping me shift the grating? It's heavy, isn't it?"

John hesitated. "We'd better leave that till dark, in case anyone notices it's gone. I'll try to get back, but if Wolf comes before I do, I think you could move it. Don't try to lift it. Just push it out flat, see? But best leave it till he actually comes. Okay?"

"All right."

"Don't worry," John said cheerfully, "everyone's far too busy upstairs to think about us at all. You'll be all right till I get back. Cheer up. Better be bored here than beaten upstairs!"

"Goodness, yes!" said Margaret. "Well, at least I'll see Wolf. You'd better go, but do be careful!"

"You bet your boots!" said John, and went.

CHAPTER THIRTEEN

It may have been pure luck, or it may—as the children ever afterwards believed—have been part of the spell that had sent them back in the nick of time to help Wolf that John should have found that very evening a chance to come near the Duke.

It was a very long chance, and no more than a chance. The children's father had often told them that luck, in life, depends largely on oneself. We are given chances, and after that it is up to us. If we have neither the courage nor the wit to grasp them and follow them up, then they are gone, and gone for ever. At least we must try. The people who never do so are those who spend an old age of regret and bitterness. Which is all to say that, late on that same evening, the chance came, and, dangerous though it was, John took it.

After he left Margaret in the secret room he made his way back towards the kitchens, and soon was plunged once more into the frantic business of fetching and carrying. He felt himself safe enough from discovery. People were recognizing him now, and calling him Hans, and not Lionel. No one had time to remember that they had not seen him before today.

It was John's turn to serve wine. It was much simpler to carry the big jug round, refilling the goblets, than it had been to run to and fro with platters of food. He had time to watch the people at the top table.

Tonight the Duke looked very regal. He wore a long robe of dark crimson, trimmed with fur, and he had a gold circlet on his head, like a crown. He still wore the amulet. Beside him sat Prince Crispin, equally splendid in amber velvet. John watched him with interest. Crispin was very like his father, and had, as Margaret had observed, the same rather pale and tired look, almost as if the same spell were working on him as on his father. Almeric, on the Duke's other side, looked alert and cheerful, and talked busily to the lady beside him. For the ladies were in the hall for the evening meal, as grandly dressed as the men, and eating just as much. Drinking, too. To John's eye, the table manners were awful. People grabbed food from the plat-

ters before they were set down, and sopped their
bread in the common dish even after they had
been chewing it. They handed each other gob-
bets of meat with their fingers, and drank from
one another's cup. If your own cup chanced to
be empty, you drank from your neighbour's yell-
ing (usually with your mouth full) for the nearest page with the wine-jug.

The manners farther up the hall were a good
deal better, and at the top table they were almost normal, but down at the kitchen end of the
hall the pages were almost run off their feet, as
men and women stuffed themselves with food,
and drank more and more, and got noisier and
noisier, until some of them even slept where
they sat, their heads on one another's shoulders,
or on the table itself, among the greasy rem-
nants of the meal.

John realized, suddenly, that the high table
was empty. The Duke had been carried out, and
his courtiers had followed. As if at a signal, the
boys and men who were serving left the hall
and crowded into the kitchens to get food for
themselves. Mindful of Margaret, he went with
them, seizing the cleanest linen napkin he could
find to wrap the food in. No one questioned him,
or seemed to think it strange that he should
want extra food. Several of the boys, he noticed,
had gone off still eating, their pouches stuffed
with sweetmeats. In the hall the men were re-
moving the tabletops from their trestles, and
shifting them with the benches back against the
walls. Dogs prowled everywhere, nosing for

scraps. People were settling down to sleep more or less where they lay. No one appeared to notice when John, with the napkin full of food, and an earthenware jug still half full of wine, left the kitchen and slipped away.

No one was about except a man who seemed to be some kind of lamplighter. He carried a long stick with a bowl at the end full of flaring tinder, and he was going from bracket to bracket along the walls of the corridors, lighting the torches for the night.

John hesitated. From what the steward had said that morning, and from the talk in the kitchens, he knew that the pages were not allowed in this part of the castle. He would have turned and gone back, and waited for the lamplighter to finish his work, but the man had seen him. To John's relief the fellow merely grinned, eyeing the napkin and the wine-jug, then winked and jerked a thumb towards the first of the cellar doors.

"He's down yonder," he said, and went off, whistling.

He? John hesitated again, but he must either go on, or go back and risk being kept in the kitchen, or made to sleep among the crowd in the hall. He let himself through the door, and hurried on.

"He" proved to be a boy of about John's own age. He was sitting on the floor beside the door of the privy, hugging his arms to his body as if in pain.

John stopped. "What's the matter?"

"Nothing," said the boy, muffled. He sat with his face turned away from John. The nearest torch was some way away, high on the wall and flaring badly, but John thought the boy looked very pale.

"What are you doing down here, then?"

"What are you doing yourself?" retorted the boy, with a flicker of spirit.

"I came to eat my supper in peace, that's all. The lamplighter thought I'd come to share it with you. Do you want some?"

He held out the napkin. At the sight of the food the boy shuddered, and his face took on a sort of greenish tinge. "No. Take it away. Leave me alone, I'm all right."

This was so obviously untrue that John ignored it. "Have you been sick or something?"

The boy nodded, keeping his face turned away. John stood, undecided. He could hardly carry the food through to the secret room while the boy was there. Besides, he looked really ill, however much he denied it. John had already seen, in the rough life of the castle, how harshly the other boys treated anyone who admitted to any sort of weakness. He sat down beside the boy.

"Look," he said kindly, "you don't have to pretend to me. I won't tell. But if you're sick, then for goodness sake have some sense and see someone about it."

The boy shook his head dumbly. John, peering closer, caught, in the unsteady light, the glimmer of a badge on the breast of his tunic.

It was a crown. Then he recognized the boy. It was the fair page in black velvet who had waited on the Duke that morning.

"Why, you're the Duke's page, aren't you?"

"Yes. I'm Justin. Who are you?"

"My name's Hans. But what *is* the matter, then? If you've been sick—" He stopped. A dreadful suspicion came suddenly into his mind. This boy would have had to taste the Duke's food and wine. John said sharply: "You must tell me what it is! Is it something you've eaten or drunk? If it is, the Duke will have to be told. You must know that."

"Yes, I know. It's not that." He looked up then, and as he turned towards the light, John saw that his face was badly marked, as if he had been in a fight. His lip was cut, and had bled freely down his chin, and the blood had dried there. There was a graze on one cheek, and one eye was rapidly blackening. It seemed likely, from the way he held himself, that he had been kicked in the stomach.

"You look as if you had been in the Crusades," said John, relieved. What he actually thought was, You look as if you've been in a rough-house, but this was how it came out, in the strange language that came so naturally to him. "What happened to the other fellow?"

"Nothing much. There were four of them. I did try, but—" Justin put his head down again. John heard a small sob, and the muttered word "coward."

"Of course you're not a coward! Anybody

would get clobbered if four bullies set on him. What had you done?"

"Nothing. Only—I'm no good at sports and all that kind of thing. The Duke chose me because I'm neat with my hands, and quiet, and because I can sing. He likes music. I didn't ask to be chosen. They call me girlish, and make mock of me. Then this afternoon I missed the quintain three times running, and they said I had to be disciplined."

"Who? The master-at-arms?" John could not help feeling thankful that he had decided to miss the "sports" that afternoon. (But maybe I'd have marked them, too, he thought grimly.)

"No. Oh, no. After he had gone," said Justin.

"I see. Well, look, even if it means telling on them, you'll have to see a physician. You needn't tell him who it was, if you're afraid to. But your father's bound to find out, isn't he? I suppose he's here?"

"No. He was taken prisoner by Count Sigismund. He hasn't been ransomed yet."

"Even so, someone's bound to guess what's happened. You can't keep out of the Duke's way for ever. As soon as he sees your face, he'll guess. The lip's swelling already, and that eye's going to be a real beauty. I didn't see you in the hall tonight, did I?"

"No. It wasn't my turn. It was Denis's. But now he's off duty, and I have to take the Duke's posset in to him. If only Denis could do it for me tonight, then perhaps by tomorrow I'd look all right, and the Duke would never guess."

He looked beseechingly at John. "You seem kind. You're not like the others. Would you find Denis for me, and ask him?"

"Wait a moment." John's heart had begun to thump. "You have to take what in to the Duke?"

"His posset. The drink he takes late at night before he sleeps. I ought to be there now, but I dare not let him see me. He'll find out who did it, and he'll punish them. And then they'll kill me, or make my life horrible—"

"Look, stop worrying, will you? I'll see to it for you, I promise. Where's Denis likely to be?"

"In the antechamber by the Duke's private stair. He'll be asleep by now, I expect."

All the better, thought John, but he did not say it aloud. He persisted with his questions, though Justin looked as if he might be sick again at any moment. "And the Duke's drink? How do you make it?"

"Denis knows," said the boy faintly. He rested his forehead on his knees again. John caught a few phrases . . . "Golden cup . . . pan for heating the milk . . . the wine he likes . . . the spices and herbs will be ready. . . ."

Oh, will they? thought John. But there was no time to wonder what would happen once he was in the Duke's private rooms and face to face with the job of mixing a posset—whatever that might be. He said quickly: "All right, I'll see to it. But if I'm to get into the private rooms to find Denis, I've got to look as if I have some right there. We'd better change clothes. Quick,

I'll help you. Mine'll be warmer for you, anyway."

He was stripping off his own tunic as he spoke. The other boy, half-dazedly, did the same, and soon John, neat in black velvet with the ducal crown on his breast, was helping Justin into his own warm tunic. As he buckled his belt back on, a thought struck him, and he quietly slipped the dagger from its hangers and tucked it into the napkin with the food. It wasn't likely that anyone would be allowed to carry arms into the Duke's presence.

"Now, do you want me to help you back into the hall? Or shall I send someone to you here?"

But Justin, full of relief and gratitude, would not hear of it. All he wanted, he said, was for John to go quickly, and find Denis. "I'd rather you went straight away, truly! I'll just go back in there for a bit, and wait till I'm better."

So John pulled him to his feet and helped him into the little room. There was a shelf above the door, and here John reached up to push the bundle of food. No time to take it to Margaret, but she would hardly need it yet.

"Look, I've hidden the food up here. If you do want some, help yourself, but don't take it all, will you? D'you want a drink of wine?"

"No, thanks."

"Then I'll take the jug with me. It'll look as if I'm running an errand. Stay there till you're better, and don't worry. I'll be back as soon as I can." He shut the door on the sick boy, then ran as fast as he could back towards the part of the castle where he knew the Duke's private rooms to be.

He found his way easily, by simply asking for Denis whenever he met anyone who was still awake and sober. But when he got to the big antechamber outside the ducal rooms he asked no more. He had his own reasons for not wanting to find Denis.

The antechamber was crowded with people. Most of these—the Duke's gentlemen—were sleeping. But men-at-arms, fully armed and alert, stood by the walls. The fire had burned low, but torches cast a fair amount of light. The room was very warm. The walls were hung with thick curtains of arras, and the air was smoky with the torches and the dying fire. At the far end of the chamber a wide, curving stair led up towards the tower room where the Duke slept.

John paused in the doorway, looking around cautiously. To his relief he could not see Denis anywhere. Clutching the wine-jug, and hoping that he looked like a page who had been sent for in a hurry, he took half a step forward into the antechamber.

Then stopped short, as he caught a movement in the shadows on the private stair. His heart lurched as he recognized Almeric. The enchanter came softly down from the Duke's rooms, and started straight across the antechamber towards the door where John was standing.

John stood rooted, his mind in a whirl. If he went on, the enchanter might stop and question

him. But it would be even more dangerous if
Almeric should see him dodge back and hide...

"Mardian!" called someone softly. Over near
the fireplace a man beckoned. The enchanter
turned, and went across to speak to him.

John pulled at the heavy folds of arras beside
the door. There was space between this and the
chamber wall. He slipped quickly into its shel-
ter. Now he could see nothing. He waited, listening. It seemed an age, but it was only a few
minutes before he heard the rushes rustling as
soft footsteps approached the doorway. The enchanter's robe brushed the arras. He neither
paused nor glanced aside. He went.

John gave him half a minute more, then
slipped out from behind the arras and ran across
the room to the stairway. There were two guards
at the foot. They made no move to stop him. One
of them said, with a grin: "Late, aren't you?
Don't blame you for dodging Lord Mardian. It's
one of those nights, so look sharp now, or the
Duke might have the skin off you, too."

John muttered something, and ran between
the two of them, and up the curving stair to the
landing outside the Duke's door.

This was the danger-point. To his immense
relief, there was no sign of Denis here, either.
But there were more guards, one to either side
of the big iron-studded door. And these two
stopped him. Their spears flashed down to cross
in front of the door, as one of them said:

"You're not Justin. Who are you?"

The other reached out, took the jug from

John's hand, and sniffed at it. "What's this? This isn't for the Duke, is it? Seems like the ordinary supper-stuff to me."

"Well, it is, but the rough red's better for heating up with the herbs and spices," said John glibly. He tried to grin, though he was very nervous. "I should know, I have to taste it for him."

The man handed it back. "Oh, aye, we know that. You're not likely to be carrying poison. But where's Justin? It's his night, isn't it?"

"Yes, but the Duke's asked for me. Seems I'm to be trained, too. I'm Hans," said John, as if that should explain everything. Then, on an inspiration, he added: "Lionel's brother. Didn't you know?"

"Lionel's brother? Now you mention it, you've got a look of him. All right, youngster, in you go. He's a bit glum tonight, I warn you, so let's hope for all our sakes that you can mix a good wine-posset."

The spears lifted. John went through. The door shut behind him. He had done it. He was in the Duke's private room.

CHAPTER FOURTEEN

Margaret, left to herself, went back to sit on the windowsill. She nibbled the marchpane, watching the deepening colour of the sky and its reflections in the moat, and waiting for the "hour between the wolf and the dog," after which Wolf-Mardian had promised to come.

Now that the drawbridge was up, there was no coming and going along the road beyond the water; no sound at all, not even the hooting of the owl.

It grew darker. The room was still warm from the day's sunlight. She found herself nodding: she had not had much sleep last night. In the end, with the stillness, and the good meal, she dozed off soundly, and did not wake until some time later, when a sound startled her out of sleep.

Wolf? She leaned towards the window. It was quite dark outside. She could see nothing, hear nothing.

John coming back? Yes, that must be it. The sound had come from beyond the door, in the big cellarage. She got up thankfully, stretching.

Then stiffened, straining to hear.

Not John. It was a heavier tread, and whoever it was cleared his throat; a man. The steward, then, or the cellarer come to tend the vats?

No, not the steward. He came straight for the secret door, and she heard his finger groping in the darkness for the knothole. The latch lifted.

No time to dislodge the grating, and clamber out of the window. And in the room itself there was only one place to hide. Opposite the door was the big cupboard, jutting from the wall. It was locked, but between it and the corner of the room was a deep recess where she could hide well enough, though any search of the room would be bound to discover her. She edged her way into the corner, past some ancient garments of leather that hung from a wooden peg. They were stiff with disuse, and they smelled rather nasty, but once she had pushed through them and steadied them from rattling, they hung in front of her, like a rotten curtain.

Not a moment too soon. The door opened, and the newcomer entered. He had a lantern with him, which threw his shadow across the floor and up the wall. For a brief moment it showed sharply against the wall opposite Margaret's corner and she recognized it. It was the wicked enchanter, Almeric.

She should have known, of course. All of them should have known. It was the one thing none of them had thought of: that if the Duke thought this was Mardian, he would assume that "Mardian" knew of the secret they had shared as boys. He must have spoken to him about the secret room. Lame as he was, the Duke could not come here himself. But it was no longer Wolf's secret. It was Almeric's, too.

Margaret's heart was beating in fast, frightened thuds.

Why had Almeric come down tonight? Did he guess, or hope, that some day Wolf might come back to the place which once he had shared with his friend? Or had he discovered John, and somehow got their secret out of him? Or perhaps, since Almeric was, after all, an enchanter, he had found out everything by his magic art. . . .

He was coming towards her corner. She held her breath. The soft footsteps stopped, and there was the sound of a key in the cupboard door. The door opened, creaking. He began to lift things from the shelves, and carry them to the table. The yellow lantern-light cast heavy shadows. He had not noticed the traces—footmarks in the dust, crumbs from the meal—that the children must have left. He had not seen, against the darkness outside, that the window

grating was not fast in its sockets. He was intent
on whatever he was doing.

There were chinking sounds, and then something that sounded like stirring, spoon on glass.
Through it all came the soft, sweet, yet terrifying sound of the enchanter humming to himself.

She could tell from the sound that he had his
back to her. Very cautiously she parted the stiff
folds of leather, and peered through.

The enchanter's tall form was bent over the
table in the center of the room. On the table
stood the things he had brought from the cupboard, flasks and bottles, a leather bag tied with
cord, a wooden box with a lock, and something
that looked like a burner with a metal tripod
over it. He had poured liquid into a big glass
flask, and was stirring this.

The lantern was smoking a little; she could
smell it, sharp and hot. It gave a strong, yellow
light. She could only hope that if John came
back now, he might see a crack of light above
the door, and be warned. And if Wolf should
come across the moat, he might be warned as
well.

At that very moment she heard it; the long
mournful howl of the great wolf in the night
outside.

The enchanter heard it, too. He lifted his
head. She ducked back, closing her peephole,
but not before she had seen his face. He was
smiling. He left the table and walked to the
window. He passed very near to Margaret. The

hanging leather garments stirred as his sleeve touched them, but he noticed nothing. He stood looking out of the window, and laughed again, softly to himself.

"Alas, my poor Mardian." The grave voice was gently mocking. Margaret's flesh crept. It was horrible to hear Mardian's own voice mocking his tragedy. "Come, then, my poor man-wolf. Come near, and let me talk to you. If I could but make you tell me where the amulet is hidden! The one thing that is lacking; the only danger...But soon this will cease to trouble me. The time is almost out, and then it will not matter that the Duke has ceased to hold 'Mardian' in his heart. Crispin will be mine, mine for long enough. I shall see that Duke Otho does not live out the moon, and once he is gone I can do what I please with the boy." Again the soft chuckle. "Oh, yes, Crispin will fall heir to much else besides the dukedom! When he has followed his father, why, then, ah, then, the dukedom will be mine, with all the wealth and power my magic masters promised me! And you, my poor wolf, will be hunted to death in my forests, by day and by night...."

The wolf howled. The sound was much nearer. Margaret listened fearfully for the noises that would tell her he was crossing the moat. But the lighted window may have warned him. He did not come, and presently the enchanter went back to the table and to his brewing.

Again the soft chanting. She risked another look. He had lighted the burner, and pushed the

trivet over it. On this was standing the flask of
liquid that he had been mixing. It was a deep
reddish-purple in colour. Almeric stirred it with
a long, pale stick that might have been made
of ivory or bone. Margaret thought that he
looked anxious. She watched, ready to duck
back again behind the folds of leather. But he
was intent on the flask as it heated over the
yellow flame.

At length, after what seemed a long time,
steam began to rise from the flask, grey steam
that curled thinly up. The liquid bubbled at the
edges. Margaret could smell the sweet, pungent
scent of it. It caught at her throat, so that she
was afraid that she might cough. The enchanter
reached to a small bag of soft leather that hung
suspended from a cord round his neck. From
this he took, so carefully that she knew it must
either be very costly or very deadly, a small
pinch of powder between thumb and forefinger.
He sprinkled this on the surface of the liquid.

Immediately the smoke changed colour. It
went white and thick, then green, green as a
slimy pool. The smell changed, and became
sweet and light, like lime flowers. Almeric
twitched the flask aside from the flame, and set
it down on the table to cool. Margaret drew back
out of sight. The enchanter came across to the
cupboard, and opened the door again. He was
moving things about on the shelves, looking for
something.

She knew that the open door of the cupboard
would hide her from him. She parted the leather

and peeped again. The flask of liquid stood there, no longer smoking. It was darker, surely, almost black, like strong medicine, or poison. . . .

A movement in it caught her eye. She watched it, puzzled. What could there be in that hot liquid? Then she realized that it was a reflection. She could see, mirrored small in the curved side of the flask, the tall figure of the enchanter, turning from the cupboard with a goblet in his hand.

And he could see her. As she shrank back again that gentle, terrifying voice spoke, with a new note in it:

"So? Whoever you are who has come into my parlour to watch and to spy, be welcome. There is a lot you can tell me before you drink this drink for me. Come out of your corner, and let us talk."

"Now," said the enchanter, "who are you?"

"If you please, my lord, my name is Gretta, and I—I was exploring."

"In the cellars? I would have thought so young a maid would have been afraid of what she might find here."

"What she might find here?" faltered Margaret. She could not help a guilty glance at the apparatus on the table, and she saw his eyes narrow, as he replied:

"Why, yes. Spiders and rats and toads and suchlike horrors."

"Oh," said Margaret.

"And in the dark, too," added Almeric gently.

Even though he looked and sounded so like Wolf-Mardian, Margaret did not need to remind herself to be afraid of him. She jumped as his voice changed. "Come now, we will have no lies. I can make you tell me the truth, be sure of that. Come here."

There was nothing for it but to obey him. She went towards him, unwillingly. She stopped a yard away, but his hand shot out and he gripped her by the arm, drawing her right up to him. His hand was very cold and his eyes looked angry. She felt herself shiver.

"Now, tell me again. Who are you and what are you doing here?"

Again, and nearer still, the wolf howled. Margaret looked down at the floor, so that he would not see her expression. She said quickly: "I am the Lady Grisel's granddaughter. I—I am not afraid of spiders, and I detest the games the other girls play, so I went exploring. I found the secret door, and there was this room. I—I tried to open the cupboard, but it was locked. I thought it would be fun to hide here. I had some marchpane, so I sat to eat it, and I fell asleep. Then I heard you coming, and I was frightened. I've run away on my own before, you see, my lord, and they caught me, and I was beaten, so—"

"As you should be beaten again," said the enchanter, smoothly. "But you are a pretty maid, and it would be a pity to hurt you. So, since you have found my secret, you shall stay here with me, and help me do my work."

She swallowed. Somehow this was a bit more frightening than his anger had been. "What work, my lord?"

He stooped his head forward, like a bird of prey. "Why, making medicine for our lord the Duke. This wolf-sickness is too slow; it is time to help our dear Duke on his way. Spells grow thin with time, little maid, and have to be renewed. So medicines must be brewed, too, from time to time, even for my Lord Mardian."

"For *Mardian*?" cried Margaret, caught off her guard.

It was a bad mistake. He did not speak, but stared at her in silence, while she felt the colour draining from her cheeks.

At last he spoke. "So. A pretty maid comes exploring, in the dark, to the secret room. A pretty maid who, it seems, knows more than she has told me. Well, my dear, you shall tell me now. Look at me."

She had to. She tilted her head up and met his eyes. And now, at last, she saw something that could never be confused with Wolf. Almeric's eyes were, indeed, the same colour as Mardian's, but where Wolf's were clear and deep and sad, the enchanter's were hard and shallow as agate stone. She saw herself reflected in them, small and distorted, as in the flask. She had the strangest feeling that she was being drawn up, up, into them, as a wisp of steam is drawn up into the sun until the pool is empty. So her mind was being drawn up from her by the power of the enchanter's eyes. Soon she would have no strength left to deceive him. She would tell him all she knew....

From the bank of the moat outside came the howl of the wolf.

The enchanter's eyes went blank. As if he had loosed her from a chain, Margaret jerked herself free of his grip, and ran towards the window. She jumped to the sill and shoved at the grating. It fell out with a crash. But that was as far as she got. The enchanter was after her in two long strides, and dragged her back into the room.

He pulled her round to face him again. To her amazement, he was laughing. "So that's it, my innocent little maid! I knew there was something about you that even I, with my magic, could not put a name to. You belong to that fool Mardian, the beast who runs in the forest.... Well, my pretty, he is running his last. It was foolish of him to use you. When he sent you here, he gave me a hostage. Or shall we say, rather, that he gave me the bait that will drag him here onto my hook?"

She could hear the sounds clearly from the moat. She struggled and kicked in the enchanter's grasp, and screamed, with all her strength:

"Run away, Wolf! It's him! He's here! Almeric's here! Run!"

The enchanter did not try to silence her. She could feel him shaking with laughter as he held her against him. She shouted again, but it was no use. Wolf was across the moat. He was coming at a plunging run up the bank through the long grass and the bushes. He was at the window. His great body blocked out the night. His fangs were bared and snarling, his eyes glaring like lamps, not yellow now, but red with a dreadful rage. He growled like an earthquake, and the great paws came scrambling over the sill.

"Run away, Wolf!" shrieked Margaret again.

"No," said the enchanter. There was a knife in his hand. He held it against Margaret's side. She gasped and stood rigid. And now he did clamp his other hand tightly across her mouth. The werwolf stopped dead, the snarl dying in his throat.

"No," repeated the enchanter. "Come in, my dear Mardian. Come in, and come quietly. Now."

CHAPTER FIFTEEN

The Duke was sitting beside a fire of logs. He had taken off his robe and crown, and was dressed in a loose-fitting furred gown and soft shoes. He was not alone. On a stool near his feet a boy sat, with his back to the door, playing a lute and singing.

The Duke seemed very tired. Far from being angry at his page's lateness, he took no notice of John at all. Nor did the singer, and for this John was very thankful, since he recognized the latter immediately. It was the page who had waited on the Duke at supper-time. Denis himself.

Once more he stood at a loss, his mind whirl-

ing as he tried to decide what to do. Denis must
have noticed Justin's absence, and taken his
place, perhaps to save him from punishment. So
had the posset already been made? If so, the
Duke would send him, John, straight away; or,
more probably, question him as soon as he saw
that the newcomer was not Justin, but a stranger.
If that happened, John would have to tell his
story, whether Denis was still there to hear it
or not. He was hardly likely to get such another
opportunity to show Wolf's amulet to the Duke.

But the Duke made no move. He sat with
head bent, staring into the fire, seemingly lost
in the music. John, whose hand was in the pouch
at his belt, clutching the precious amulet, now
let it drop back into its hiding place, and looked
around him. He noticed two things: there was
no cup on the small inlaid table beside the
Duke's chair, and at the other side of the room,
hidden from both Denis and his master by a tall
carved screen, stood a table with all the apparatus for the posset, with a golden chalice standing empty and waiting.

So the Duke's drink had not yet been prepared. John tiptoed quickly across to the table.
Beside the chalice he saw a bowl of milk, and
a copper pan with a long handle, for heating the
milk at the fire. A tall gilded jug held wine, and
there were a great many jars and carved wooden
boxes. The spices and herbs, he thought uneasily, eyeing them, and wondering where, among
all these complicated ingredients, Almeric's

poison lurked, and how he contrived that the two pages should not suffer from it.

But he did not waste much thought on this. He had had time to think now, and realized that he need not, in fact, mix the posset at all. The Duke was not likely to notice the drink when once he had the chalice in his hands. For there was one way in which John could hand him the amulet without even Denis seeing it....

The screen hid him from the others in the room. He took the amulet from his pouch and dropped it silently into the empty chalice. Over it he poured just enough of the wine from his own jug to hide it. The rest of the wine went into the copper pan. He did not touch the gilded jug, or the bowl of milk.

The song seemed to be coming to an end. Perhaps now Denis would be sent away. John lingered, shifting things about on the table, and making discreet mixing noises.

The last note faded. The Duke said: "Thank you," then, raising his voice a little, "Justin? Make haste to heat the drink, boy. It grows late.... That last stave again, Denis, so please you."

The notes rippled. The boy's voice rose again. There was nothing for it. He would have to pretend to mix the drink. John ran his hands quickly over his hair, gave a tug to Justin's tunic, then carried pan and chalice over to the hearth.

He set the chalice down. There was an iron trivet to one side of the fireplace, and on that he put the copper pan to heat. Keeping his face turned to the fire, he knelt there on the hearth, holding the pan by its long handle, and trying to control the sharp beating of his heart. The fire burned against his face, but he was shivering with nerves and excitement.

The wine in the pan was bubbling at the edges. John withdrew the pan from the flames and poured a little of the hot stuff into the cup. His hand was shaking. Some of the wine spilled.

A string of the lute twanged harshly, out of tune. In the middle of a phrase, the music stopped. The Duke looked up.

Denis said breathlessly: "My lord! This boy! This is not Justin, and he's not one of the pages. I've never seen him before!"

The Duke said: "So? Who are you, boy?"

John set the pan back on the hearth, and got to his feet. He turned, with the golden cup held carefully between his hands.

The Duke looked him up and down. His eyes were cold. "Well?"

"My Lord," John began, hurriedly. "Justin was ill, and asked me to send Denis to you instead. But I could not see him anywhere, so—"

"I asked who you were."

"My name is Hans," began John, but the other boy interrupted him. He had jumped to his feet and gone over to the table, pushing back the screen.

"He's made your drink with his own wine, my lord! He hasn't used the milk, and the herb boxes and jars haven't been touched! Look, here's the jug he brought with him. It wasn't here before."

All at once the Duke did not look sad or tired at all. He sat up straight in his chair, and his eyes went to the earthenware jug standing on the table among the silver and gold and carved wood. Then he shouted aloud:

"Guard! Ho, there, guard!"

The door swung open. The two guards came running in. At a gesture from the Duke they closed in, one to either side of John, and held him fast.

"Don't let him spill the wine," said the Duke sharply.

John had not moved. It had all happened too quickly. The wine rocked in the cup, but it did not spill. The Duke put an elbow on the arm of his chair, and sat, chin on fist, regarding John in silence. It was a rather frightening silence.

John licked his lips. They were very dry. It was now or never, in spite of the presence of Denis and the guards. But before he could say anything the Duke spoke again, coldly. "Is it true that you are a stranger to my court?"

"Yes, my lord."

"Then I think you had better begin by telling me who you are, and where you come from. Who is your father?"

There was a kind of relief, at last, in telling the simple truth. "You would not know him, sir. It is true that I don't come from this dukedom, but this does not matter, truly. I'll tell you everything, but you will understand it better if first of all you will let me give you the message that I bring from the Lord Mardian."

The Duke frowned. "From Mardian? Why, he was here only a few minutes ago. What nonsense is this? What sort of message? He sent you with that jug of wine?"

"No, I—I brought the wine myself." John hesitated, wondering how to go on. It was hard to think, with the men's hands gripping his arms, and the Duke's icy grey eyes boring into his. Wolf had insisted that the amulet must be put straight into the Duke's hands, in private. Could he really hand it to him here, in front of the guards and the boy?

Then he jumped as the Duke said, to one of the guards: "Go and send to find my Lord Mardian, and beg him to come here."

"*No!*" cried John.

The man checked, halfway to the door. The Duke signed to him to stay where he was. "I thought so. What sort of message do you bring, that Mardian could not give me himself? Or that you dare not repeat in front of him?"

There was obviously no help for it. "The message is in the wine," cried John.

"I'm sure it is," said the Duke drily. "A message from Count Sigismund, perhaps?"

"No, no! If you would only take it—!" But when he tried to thrust the chalice forward towards the Duke, the guard's grip tightened on his arm, so roughly that he cried out.

The man said hoarsely: "There's something

in the cup, my lord! You can see it, under the wine!"

The Duke's brows went up, though he did not look surprised. He had not glanced at the man. He kept staring at John. "The message, no doubt? Well, Hans, you have brought it here. Now deliver it in a seemly way."

"Sir?" stammered John, not understanding, but beginning to feel really frightened. The guard still held him so that he could not move.

"Perhaps you had forgotten," said the Duke, "that my pages taste my wine before my cup is given to me? Yes, I thought you had. Let him go." This to the guard, who released John's arm. "Now, drink," commanded the Duke.

John's heart was beating wildly, but through the fear came relief. He had quite forgotten the tasting. At least he could prove that the wine was not poisoned, and then, surely, the Duke would ask to see what was within the cup? Without a second's hesitation he lifted the chalice to his mouth.

But before the wine could do more than wet his lips the Duke spoke again, one word, and the cup, struck from John's hand by the guard, went spinning to the floor. The wine splashed out across the boards. The amulet flew, ringing, into the firelight.

There was a sudden, complete silence. The Duke, still as death in his chair, stared down at the amulet. The singer, the two guards, never moved. Then the Duke's hand crept up to touch

the golden token that hung still at his breast.
He looked up at John.

"Sir," said John breathlessly. "That was the
message. May I talk to you now, please?"

The Duke did not once interrupt as John told
his story. At a sign from him, Denis had picked
up the amulet, and all the time John talked the
Duke held Mardian's amulet in his hand, turning it over and over, so that the firelight caught
the lettering: OTHO—FIDELIS—OTHO. The guards
had moved away, and stood beside the door.

John came to the end of his story. "And my
sister's down there now, in the secret room that
Wolf showed us. Wolf—Mardian—promised to
come back there every night if he could. He
might be there now. If you would only come
down, my lord..." He swallowed. "You see, he
has to stay a wolf till daybreak, but if only you
were there, and could wait till dawn, and would
stop anyone killing him or harming him, you
would see the change, and know it was all true.
I don't know what will happen, my lord, or how
Almeric's spells can be broken, but it must be
true that they can be broken somehow, or why
have my sister and I been brought here, and
why has everything happened like this?" And
he looked round at the gaping Denis, the waiting guards, the firelit chamber with the spilt
wine on the floor.

There was a pause. The Duke had not once
taken his eyes from John's face. It was impos-
sible to tell what he was thinking, or if he be-

lieved a word of the story. John found that he was trembling. If the Duke did not believe him, if Wolf did not come, who knew what kind of harsh fate might be waiting for Margaret and himself? They had been brought here to break the spell; if they did not succeed, would they ever get back safely into their own world and their own time?

The Duke's hand clenched suddenly, tightly, on Mardian's amulet. He turned to the guards. There was no sign now of fatigue or sickness. His voice was crisp and hard.

"Call the captain on duty, and wake my gentlemen. The servants, too, to carry my chair. We will go down now to this room in the cellarage, and see if we may learn the truth of this strange tale." He turned to Denis. "And you, see that the wine in the golden jug, and all the mixings for the posset, are kept for my physicians to examine. Now, does anyone know where my Lord Mardian is? The man—as this boy would say—whom we know as my Lord Mardian?"

No one did. The cold eyes came back to John. "You have told me a strange tale, of sorcery and violence and treachery. Because of this amulet, which is the sign of trust and faithfulness, I have listened to you, and I am prepared to believe that what you tell me may be true. But I cannot proceed against my Lord Mardian, whom you call Almeric, without proof. If the great wolf of Wolfenwald is indeed a werwolf, condemned by sorcery, then he must yield himself to our mercy until this tale be proved true, or else shown to be lies."

"Oh, he will, he will!" cried John. "Just wait till daylight, and don't let them kill him, and then you'll see! Please, Lord Duke, let's all go straight down to the cellar, now!"

In a moment all was noise and hurrying. The door was thrown open, and one of the guards went shouting for the Duke's captain and his soldiers. Denis ran to stand guard over the table with the wine and spices. Someone came running with his master's sword, and knelt to gird it on. Servants hurried in with poles, which they threaded through sockets at the sides of the Duke's chair. Torches were brought, there were shouted commands, and the orderly tramp of feet.

Suddenly, through all the noise, could be heard a shrill cry, and a boy came running. It was Justin, the bruises showing black on his pale face.

"My lord, my lord! There's a great wolf in the cellarage, and my Lord Mardian is there with it! I was in the privy chamber, and I heard him go by. Then I heard voices, and went to look through the cellar door, and saw Lord Mardian, with a young girl, and a knife in his hand, protecting her with his life against a wolf! My lord, it was the great wolf himself!"

CHAPTER SIXTEEN

Down in the secret room the dreadful moment seemed to last for ever. Wolf crouched just inside the window, rigid as a statue, the snarl frozen on his jaws. Margaret could not move at all; Almeric's hand gripped her so tightly against him that she could hardly breathe. In his other hand the knife gleamed.

The enchanter seemed quite calm. She could feel the steady beat of his heart against her. He spoke to Wolf.

"Keep your distance! Yes, that's it. Stay exactly there. If you make any move towards me, or if you try to escape through that window, I think you know what will happen to this child. Yes?"

Wolf snarled, and stayed just where he was. Almeric laughed. "What a good beast it is! And you, child—did you say your name was Gretta?— if I take my hand from your mouth, you will make no sound. Is that understood?"

Margaret managed to nod. The hard hand moved, but his grip on her remained. She made no attempt to cry out again, and the enchanter nodded his approval. "Good, good. How very sensible."

"They wouldn't hear me anyway," said Margaret. Her voice sounded hoarse and sullen. She rubbed at her sore lips.

"No. And even if they did, and came here to look for you, they would listen to me, rather than to you, and they would certainly do my bidding, and kill your friend the werwolf. How right you are, my pretty dear! And I was right, too, about you, was I not? You belong to the wolf, and he sent you here. Well, we shall go presently, you and I, where you can talk to me and tell me all I want to know. But first to cage this wild beast up fast, to wait for our sport with him."

Margaret did cry out at that. Wolf did not stir. She could see that she was indeed a hostage; while the enchanter held her in his grip, the werwolf would do exactly as he was bidden, even if it meant his death.

There was no point any longer in pretending. Margaret spoke breathlessly, straight to him.

"Wolf, dear, run away now! It's all right! He can't really hurt me, you know! It's just a dream, or a spell! You know it is!! All I have to do now is wake up, so go now, quickly! *Please*, Wolf!"

She did half believe, half hope, that this was true, but it was still very brave of her to say it, with the enchanter's grip on her feeling very real indeed, and the enchanter's laughter in her ear. And when Wolf made no move at all, she could not help the swift relief that swept through her.

Almeric had stiffened as she spoke. Now he nodded with satisfaction. "Yes. I thought you would see it my way, Mardian the werwolf! So now, since this chamber holds secrets that I would like to keep secret, you, wolf, will go ahead of us out into the big cellar....Slowly, now, slowly, if you wish the little maid to stay unhurt...Now, wait where I can see you, at the end of the cellar, away from the stairs. Yes, there. Now stay! Stay! Lie down!"

All the time he was talking he himself was moving after Wolf, out of the secret room. He edged carefully between the wine vats, reaching out swiftly to pull the door shut behind them. Margaret heard the latch drop. Now, whatever happened, Wolf could not escape without someone to lift the latch for him. He was caged, like a beast. And what made it all extra horrible was that Almeric, when he spoke to him, used the kind of voice that people sometimes use to dogs. Margaret, scared as she was, still felt herself flushing with shame and rage. She had a

sharp impulse to hack Almeric on the shins, but
managed to stop herself when she saw how Wolf,
even as he obeyed the harsh commands, showed
a kind of dignity. He moved quietly to the cellar's end and lay down, head on paws, like a
waiting lion. Though his eyes still had a watchful glare, and his ears were flat to his skull, he
looked calm, and his calmness helped her.

Almeric, too, was watchful. It was obvious
that he dared not make even the smallest mistake. Slowly, still holding Margaret, he began
to back the length of the cellar towards the stone
stairway.

As he went, he talked. "Now, as you see, my
dear Gretta, your friend the werwolf cannot escape...not, that is, until he resumes his man's
shape, and has a hand to unfasten the latch.
And well before that time I shall have called
my friends hither, and we shall do the dukedom
a service in ridding it of the plague of Wolfenwald....Quietly, now! If you kick me, be sure
I shall hurt you. And be sure, my pretty maid,
that if this *is* a dream, you are caged in it as
fast as your Wolf is in his cellar!"

"Where are you taking me?" She wanted to
sound brave again, but her voice was thin and
a bit squeaky with fright.

"To my own chamber, where I shall have lei-
sure to question you, without having to keep
watch on the wolf all the while."

"I shan't tell you anything! There's nothing
to tell!"

"Two statements, neither of which is true,"

he said calmly. "Have you stopped being sensible? The werwolf must have told you his story, and you know who I am. You also found out, in the secret room yonder, that I have the power to make you tell me anything I want to know. And since you spied on my work there, you will also know that I have, in this pouch here on my breast, a magic powder with which to work—or to renew—the wolf-spell. Mardian needs it no longer; he will be dead before dawn; but how would you, little Gretta, like to take his place?"

"*No!*"

From his smile she thought—hoped—that he was only trying to frighten her still more. She was trying desperately to think. There was no point in hanging back, or talking to delay him; there were hours yet to go to daybreak, when Wolf could become a man again; and long before that Almeric would make sure that he was killed. But—and it was a big "but"—the enchanter obviously did not know or suspect anything about John. If only he could be got out of the way before John came down to the cellar, then John would be able to let Wolf out, and the two of them could come to her rescue through the sleeping castle. And then at last Wolf would have the chance to tackle his enemy, and perhaps break the spell.

"All right," she said sullenly. "What do you want me to tell you?"

"About the charm."

"What charm?" They were halfway along the cellar now. Still Wolf had not moved, except that his head was up, and the glare had gone from his eyes. His ears, which had been laid flat back, were erect, as if he was listening to something outside the cellar.

Behind her, at the head of the stairway, she thought she heard a faint sound, as if the great door had opened. Her heart lurched with fright. John! She risked a swift glance over her shoulder. Nothing. The door was shut. "What charm?" she asked again, rather wildly.

Almeric gave her a sharp little shake. "Try not to be stupid! The amulet, Gretta, the amulet! The amulet that no doubt Mardian has entrusted to you to bring into the hands of Duke Otho. The silly boyhood gift with its silly motto, that alone could make Otho listen to a tale as wild as any child's bedtime story, of werwolves and magic and moonshine! Why else are you here? Why else would Duke Otho ever lend an ear to you, a child? You have the amulet, Gretta, or you know where it is. So tell me. Where?"

"Oh, that thing! I didn't know it was a charm. I haven't got it."

"Are you still trying to pretend to me?" he said angrily.

"No, oh, no! What would be the use? I only meant I haven't got it on me. I hid it."

They had almost reached the foot of the stairway. She went thankfully. Perhaps after all they would be out of the way when John came. But first she must let Wolf know where to find her.

She turned his way, to see with some alarm that he was on his feet now, standing with ears erect and head cocked slightly to one side. She knew that look. It was the way Tray stood when he could hear (or smell or see) something not perceptible to humans. She raised her voice, talking quickly and loudly so that Wolf could hear her clearly, and John, if he was approaching the door, would be warned that something was wrong.

"Lord Almeric, you've guessed that the wolf brought me here, and bade me give the amulet into the Duke's hands. That was last night. But I couldn't come near the Duke, only to the women's rooms, *and so, Lord Almeric—*"

"Stop shouting!" snapped the enchanter. "And so?"

"After dinner," gabbled Margaret, without lowering her voice at all, "when we were in the garden—that's the upper garden where the girls play—I hid it below a bush. *I buried it, Lord Almeric!*"

They had reached the stairs now. Carefully, watching Wolf all the time, Almeric began to back up them.

"Which bush?"

"The third, I think, or was it the fourth? Not far along from the little urn. I—"

"Which urn?"

"Is there more than one? I don't remember. But I could find it if we went there now. Lord Almeric—"

Then she heard what Wolf had heard seconds

before. A sound in the corridor beyond the great door. Someone coming, with no secrecy at all. John had not heard her. Here he came, with the precious amulet still in the pouch at his belt, ready for Almeric to take, and destroy them all!

She drew a sharp breath of terror, and screamed as loudly as she could:

"*No, no, no! He's here, Almeric's here! Almeric's here!*"

The hand clamped across her mouth again, cutting off the scream. In the same moment, she realized that it was not just one person approaching, but a whole crowd of people. They were not jostling and talking like an ordinary crowd, but coming swiftly and in order, like a troop of soldiers.

And that, when the door opened and she strained round to look, was exactly what she saw.

CHAPTER SEVENTEEN

To the Duke's soldiers and gentlemen, Margaret's cry seemed to echo what Justin had just told them. There, on the steps of the cellarage, stood the man they knew as Mardian, with a girl clasped to him, facing the menacing crouch of the great wolf. He was armed only with a knife, and the girl had been screaming with terror—something about Almeric. Some of those present thought, like Crispin, that the wolf might indeed be the missing Almeric.

Almeric himself, though taken by surprise at the sudden clamour at the door, recovered himself quickly. Keeping his hand tightly across

Margaret's mouth, he backed a step higher, calling breathlessly:

"A rescue! A rescue! The beast broke in from the moat, and would have killed this child!" To the newcomers, pressing in through the doorway in the wake of the Duke's chair, it looked as if he were protecting her with his own body. "It's the great wolf himself!" cried Almeric. "Kill him now, and rid the land of this most accursed plague!"

There was the whine of steel as swords whipped out. John shouted desperately: *"No!"* and at the same moment the Duke's voice rang out, clear and commanding:

"Stop! Put up your swords!"

At the sound of the Duke's voice three things happened. Almeric, starting violently, whirled round to face his master. He relaxed his hold of Margaret, who broke free. Wolf, in swift and deadly silence, bunched his great muscles to launch himself at last towards his enemy.

What might have happened then it was hard to guess. If Wolf had actually sprung on Almeric, one of the swords would surely have caught and cut him down. But Margaret, shrieking: *"No, Wolf, no!"* ran, not away from the dreadful beast, but straight to him, and flung herself on her knees beside him, with both arms clasped tightly round his neck.

And the great wolf of Wolfenwald stopped short in his tracks. The bristling hair flattened along his back. The red glare died from his eyes. His head went down. As the servants set the

Duke's chair at the foot of the steps, Wolf sank to the floor in front of it, and laid his head at his master's feet.

Into the awed silence, Almeric said hoarsely: "Sorcery! This is evil sorcery! The girl is a witch! I found her at the table in that room yonder— our room, Otho! You may see the potions and spells she was concocting! You need look no further for the cause of your ailments!"

"Sorcery indeed," said the Duke, "and certainly evil. Well, we shall soon prove the truth of it." He spoke to Margaret kindly. "Come here to me, child."

Margaret stood up. Her legs were shaking. She went and stood by John, near the Duke's chair. John murmured under his breath: "He has it. He'll believe us. It'll be all right, you'll see."

The children stood rather close together, holding hands. All at once their adventure— whether dream or spell or reality—had changed, like moving into different air, and had become something solemn and splendid and terrible. There sat the Duke in his gilded chair, wrapped in his cloak of royal scarlet. He had looked nowhere except at the great wolf lying at his feet. His face was very pale, but composed and stern. When he spoke, he did not raise his voice, but his words fell into such a silence that you would have thought every man there was holding his breath.

He spoke at last, with courtesy to Almeric. "My lord, you also have been accused of sorcery.

No, be silent now. You will, with this beast, and
with these children, stand trial of it soon." Then
he spoke straight to Wolf, at his feet. "And you,
if you are truly what these children would have
me believe, you need fear nothing. But my people fear you, so, until the truth is known, you
will let them bind you, while we wait for morning. Bring the chains and bind them both."

At this, the false enchanter began to protest,
but already the soldiers were holding him. They
bound his wrists together with chains—gently,
for to them this was still the Lord Mardian,
friend of Duke Otho. Those who approached the
wolf did so nervously, but he never stirred, and
presently they had him shackled with heavy
chains. Because they were afraid of him, and
perhaps because they were still afraid of Almeric, they used him roughly. The children
watched, distressed, until they saw how the
Duke watched, too, with something in his face
that had not been there before. And all the time,
hidden in his hand, he held the amulet.

When the chains were fast, he spoke again.
"Now we will go up to the terrace garden, to
wait for daybreak. The children will stay with
me."

It was still dark outside. They all trooped up
to the terrace where Margaret had first seen
Almeric with the prince. The servants carrying
the torches ranged themselves back against the
wall of the upper garden. The smoke from the
torches drifted upwards through the overhang-
ing myrtle bushes. A pair of sleepy peacocks,

roosting there, stirred, protesting, then fled squawking at the sight of Wolf. There were little orange trees, in tubs, set along beside the low outer battlement. They smelled rich and sweet. There was no wind, and the grass was heavy with dew.

The servants set the Duke's chair down facing the battlement. In front of him, beside the orange trees, Almeric and the wolf stood face to face in their chains. No one spoke. Time passed. Almeric did turn, once, towards the Duke, as if to speak, but Otho said quietly: "Friend, of your courtesy, be silent now until the test is made. In a trial of faith, what has the true Mardian to fear? Afterwards, if you are indeed my friend, we shall speak together, and I promise you that your recompense shall be great."

The enchanter could do nothing but fall silent. But his fettered hands were clenched against his breast, and his lips moved, as if trying, even here, for a spell.

Somewhere, down in the distant village, a cock crowed.

Wolf lifted his head. His chains clanked. Almeric made a sharp movement, as if of sudden fear.

The children looked at one another. They were both remembering, in the same moment, the change that had taken place in the cottage. They thought of Wolf's shame then, and his talk of "suffering." The change from wolf to man might not be so dreadful and humiliating as the

one they had overheard, but they remembered
something else about it.

"Go on," whispered Margaret. "Tell him."

John leaned forward, and spoke briefly, under
his breath, to the Duke. The Duke smiled, and
without hesitation lifted the cloak of royal scarlet, lined with fur, which his gentlemen had
thrown round him against the chill of the night
air. He handed it to John, who ran to where
Wolf stood, and threw it over him, so that only
his head showed.

The cock crowed again. They had put the
torches out a while ago. The stars were fainter.
The sky was changing colour.

The night-time clouds thinned, became grey
smoke, broke up like ripples on a quiet shore.
And over the ripples, brushing their edges with
gold, washing through and over them with
waves of light, came day.

And then, at last, the sun.

It shone full on the terrace, right in the eyes
of the assembled people. For a few moments
they could see nothing, then, all in the blink of
a dazzled eye, it happened.

The chains fell, clanging, from Almeric, from
Wolf...

There was no Wolf. Where Wolf had stood
there was Mardian, tall and upright, clothed in
the dignity of the royal mantle. A pace from
him, like a reflection seen in a glass, stood the
false Mardian, his hands clutching in sudden
terror at the little leather bag that was hung
round his neck. It could be seen that the chains,

in falling, had torn the soft leather, and there, trickling and then pouring from the bag, came a white powder as fine as sand. It ran down his robe, over his feet, over the hands that, scrabbling to stop it, clutched and curled like claws. He was mouthing something that did not sound like words at all. The powder spattered on the dewy grass. Where it fell, the dew began to smoke.

For a few moments of time the two Mardians stood there, face to face. Then the enchanter, throwing up his head, gave a great cry that changed to something like a howl. As the company stared in horror, he seemed to shrink, then to shrivel and fall on the grass at Mardian's feet.

"Seize him!" commanded the Duke. The men-at-arms leaped forward, but found themselves grabbing at empty air. There was nothing but a patch of burnt grass with a pile of clothes, and the enchanter's long knife. Down below in the moat something splashed, swimming. A grey shape slunk ashore on the far bank, and fled away into the darkness of Wolf Wood.

The astonished silence was broken by a sudden clamour. Prince Crispin, newly risen from bed, with a dozen or so companions of his own age, came racing and clattering along the terrace. They were dressed for riding, and carried bows and spears and hunting horns. "To the hunt!" they shouted. They crowded excitedly to the battlements, pointing and exclaiming. "There! Did you see it? No, not there, farther

over. There he is! The wolf himself! We shall have good sport today! To horse, to horse!"

Their shouts died to muttering, and the muttering to silence. No one was taking the slightest notice of them. For there, in front of the chair that had carried him for five weary years, Duke Otho stood upright and smiling. At his feet knelt Mardian, his hands between those of his friend. Then the Duke raised him, saluting him with a kiss, and solemnly, as if it were a ceremony—which of course it was—hung round Mardian's neck, once more, the amulet marked FAITHFUL.

At this a great shout went up. Men who only half understood, but who had seen enough to know they had witnessed wonders, clasped one another and laughed and shouted. The Duke and Mardian stood holding one another's hands, and smiling.

"Father!" cried Prince Crispin. "Are you cured?" Then, when no one answered or even looked at him: "Will someone kindly tell me what is going on? Mardian? What's happened, Mardian? *Mardian!*"

But Mardian could only shake his head, for once again—but with very different tears—he was weeping.

FAREWELL

The children walked out across the drawbridge. Below them the moat glimmered in the rich light of late afternoon. They were sleepy from the feasting, and half dazed with happiness and the splendour of the celebrations in the castle. They reached the roadway. Ahead of them rose the trees of Wolfenwald, green in the sunlight. They turned to look back.

Mardian was standing at the other end of the bridge, in the center of the great gateway. He lifted a hand in salute. Behind him the castle stood, sunlit and solid, fluttering with flags and alive with music and rejoicing. The Duke's standard flew from the tallest tower.

From the direction of Wolf Wood a voice was calling them by name: their father's.

"Margaret! John!" And there he was, coming down the road towards them. "Time to go!" he called.

They ran to meet him. The tarmacadam of the road was hot, sweating in the heat. The sun flashed from the windscreen of the parked car. Behind them the ruined castle lifted its empty turrets to the afternoon sky.

ABOUT THE AUTHOR

MARY STEWART, one of the most popular novelists writing today, was born in Sunderland, County Durham, England. She received a B.A. with first class honours in English Language and Literature from Durham University and went on for her M.A. Later she returned to her own University as a Lecturer in English.

Mary Stewart's career as a novelist began in 1954 with the publication of *Madam, Will You Talk?* Since then she has published fifteen successful novels, including *The Last Enchantment* (1979), the third book of her trilogy about the legendary enchanter Merlin and young Arthur. In 1968, she was elected Fellow of the Royal Society of the Arts.

CLASSIC BESTSELLERS
from FAWCETT BOOKS

☐ MAGGIE: A GIRL OF THE STREETS   30854 $2.25
   by Stephen Crane
☐ SATAN IN GORAY   24326 $2.50
   by Isaac Bashevis Singer
☐ THE RISE AND FALL OF THE
     THIRD REICH   23442 $3.95
   by William Shirer
☐ THE WIND   04579 $2.25
   by Dorothy Scarborough
☐ ALL QUIET ON THE WESTERN FRONT   23808 $2.50
   by Erich Maria Remarque
☐ TO KILL A MOCKINGBIRD   08376 $2.50
   by Harper Lee
☐ NORTHWEST PASSAGE   24095 $2.95
   by Kenneth Roberts
☐ THEM   23944 $2.95
   by Joyce Carol Oates
☐ THE FLOUNDER   24180 $2.95
   by Gunter Grass
☐ THE CHOSEN   24200 $2.95
   by Chaim Potok
☐ THE SOURCE   23859 $3.50
   by James A. Michener

Buy them at your local bookstore or use this handy coupon for ordering.

COLUMBIA BOOK SERVICE
32275 Mally Road, P.O. Box FB, Madison Heights, MI 48071

Please send me the books I have checked above. Orders for less than 5 books must include 75¢ for the first book and 25¢ for each additional book to cover postage and handling. Orders for 5 books or more postage is FREE. Send check or money order only.

Cost $_____   Name _____

Sales tax*_____   Address _____

Postage _____   City _____

Total $_____   State _____ Zip _____

*The government requires us to collect sales tax in all states except AK, DE, MT, NH and OR.

This offer expires 1 March 82   8178

FAWCETT COLUMBINE
SCIENCE FICTION & SCIENCE FACT

Large-format books by the masters of the genre.

☐ EXTRATERRESTRIAL CIVILIZATIONS   90020 $5.95
By Isaac Asimov
"The question is: Are we alone?" Isaac Asimov believes we are not alone. A thorough investigation of the possibilities of life elsewhere in the universe.

☐ ISAAC ASIMOV'S BOOK OF FACTS   90034 $6.95
By Isaac Asimov
A fascinating conglomeration of facts spanning practically every subject imaginable. 3,000 interesting and unusual bits of information presented in almost 100 different categories.

☐ THE NUMBER OF THE BEAST   90019 $6.95
By Robert A. Heinlein
Four sensual geniuses suddenly find themselves the target of alien hostilities and are forced to flee their universe. A beautifully illustrated new masterwork by the author of STRANGER IN A STRANGE LAND.

☐ TOWARD DISTANT SUNS   90035 $8.95
By T.A. Heppenheimer
A boldly illustrated study of the future of space colonization. Dr. Heppenheimer examines the plans for human settlement in other parts of the solar system from space shuttles to space industrialization.

Buy them at your local bookstore or use this handy coupon for ordering.

COLUMBIA BOOK SERVICE (a CBS Publications Co.)
32275 Mally Road, P.O. Box FB, Madison Heights, MI 48071

Please send me the books I have checked above. Orders for less than 5 books must include 75¢ for the first book and 25¢ for each additional book to cover postage and handling. Orders for 5 books or more postage is FREE. Send check or money order only.

Cost $_____   Name _____

Sales tax*_____   Address _____

Postage_____   City _____

Total $_____   State _____ Zip _____

* *The government requires us to collect sales tax in all states except AK, DE, MT, NH and OR.*

This offer expires 1 February 82   **8167**

Attention: Schools and Corporations

FAWCETT books are available at quantity discounts with bulk purchase for educational, business, or sales promotional use. For more information and a catalog write to:

EDUCATION AND SPECIAL SALES DEPT.
FAWCETT BOOKS GROUP
1515 BROADWAY
NEW YORK, NY 10036

Attention: Individual Readers

Are there FAWCETT books you want to read but cannot find in your local bookstore? You can order any FAWCETT title in print by completing the order form below, attaching it to your list of selections, and mailing both with your payment to the address indicated:

COLUMBIA BOOK SERVICE
P.O. BOX FB, 32275 MALLY RD.
MADISON HEIGHTS, MI 48071

Please send book(s) selected. Orders for less than 5 books must include 75¢ for first book and 25¢ for each additional book to cover postage and handling. Postage and handling are FREE on orders of 5 books or more. Send check or money order only.

Cost	$_____	Name_____
Sales tax*	_____	Address_____
Postage	_____	City_____
Total	_____	State_____Zip_____

☐ **8461** Check here if you wish Columbia Book Service catalog sent. Add 50¢ to help defray postage and handling costs.

*The government requires us to collect sales tax in all states except AK, DE, MT, NH and OR.